SEDUCED *by a* PREDATOR

The Double Life of Annabelle

Seduced
BY A PREDATOR

The Double Life of Annabelle

a novel by

MICHELE GMITROWSKI

Who would think that life could go from such a strict upbringing, growing up naïve and living such a simple, sheltered life, would end up in such horrific circumstances?

My family raised me to be a 'good girl,' the word 'boyfriend' was a dirty word, and I never had the 'talk' about sex, babies, and how the reproductive procedure works, and god forbid I ever found out!

Yes, that's how it was. I guess I believed that it was healthy and respected raised that way until I graduated high school. Before I graduated, so many others the same age as me had been at school for those health classes for sex education. I just happened to miss those classes for some reason, unfortunately. The day I got my period, I almost felt ashamed to bring it up to my mother, but of course, I had no choice and was handed what I needed and figured the rest out for myself. Parents openly talked with them about sex and felt ok to speak of it in front of others. I just went along with everyone and pretended that I knew what he or she was talking about, giggled, and laughed to make the others think I knew everything. What else was I supposed to do? It was embarrassing, and I just wanted so badly to fit in and feel like everybody else.

It was a pretty scary world out there once high school was over, and it came down to looking for a job. I never felt good enough to go to college or university and was never pushed to do it. I was only 17, had long black hair down to my waist, and weighed 105lbs. I never thought or saw myself as being a pretty girl, and when complemented, I found it hard to accept and usually laugh it off. Going for job interviews, it seemed, when being interviewed by a woman, I didn't seem good enough for the job and always seemed to get a dirty look. When it came to men talking to me, they never looked me in the face but found it ok to stare at my breasts, not that they were popping out of my dress or anything, but it made me extremely uncomfortable. If you didn't play along, you didn't get the job.

Well, I finally got my first part-time job at the offices of a Kodak photo developing company. Although it was a part-time job, I'll admit that not knowing anyone there and walking into a strange building scared me. I was sent there through a job agency that I signed through.

I proceeded to this small office, where I would be working by myself, and it was filing, but not the kind I thought I knew. It was going through photographs that were not allowed and were of people who had taken of themselves naked. I guess in those days, as this was going back to the seventies, it wasn't allowed to print those photos in stores or given to the individuals who took them. I couldn't believe some of the images I came across, such as one particular couple that took photos of them doing housework completely naked. There was nothing pornographic about them in any way. However, nude photographs were against company policies and could not be sold back to these individuals by companies such as this, and files made for them.

I wish somebody had told me what this job entailed. I must admit I did get a giggle as the photos were just so silly. Why would anyone use an entire roll of film on something like that? I guess it's to each their own, although it just seemed bizarre to me with my innocence. And I had to work there for three days, which I must admit after the first day seemed rather dull. I had no choice but to get some experience under my belt before applying for other jobs.

The next job I applied for was at a bank where a written test, along with a typing test, was on an actual typewriter. No, computers didn't exist yet in offices, we even used manual calculators.

Along came another part-time job, and it was for the Bank, but one of their branches in ChinaTown. I didn't have a car, so those days relied on buses and subways. Not to sound racist, but when I took the streetcar to this particular job, all I can remember to this day is a lot of clearing of throats, snorting, spitting and coughing. It was disgusting and made me feel slightly sick. Anyway, I finally got to the branch; I met the Administration Manager, who took me over to a desk with a huge stack of letters and another stack of envelopes. Yes, you guessed it, my job was to put the letters into these envelopes and seal each one, but hey, I had to start somewhere, as this was the Bank I was where I wanted to work. I spent two days at this job and was happy when it was over.

I was beginning to wonder if I would get a regular job where I could feel useful in more ways than what I had done so far. Then I finally had a call to go for an interview at another branch of this Bank, but this time it was downtown in the city, and it was for a Clerk position. I did the required test, had my interview with this very peculiar man who was the Administration Manager, but with all the stares during the meeting, I tried to ignore them as this was my chance to get a foot in the door of this Bank.

Well, I got the job and was very excited, as it was

my first full-time job making just over $7,000.00 a year, which seemed like so much money to me back then. The post had more responsibilities. I typed letters for the Administrator as he is who I reported to; I helped customers who came in with inquiries and directed them to the right people and answered the phone, which I had on my desk, yes, an office that was all mine!

I grew up in England, and still had my accent that seemed appealing to many people. The way I answered the phone was excellent, polite, and helpful to one of my assets. My typing was excellent, and those were the days when we used sheets of carbon paper to make a carbon copy for someone if required. We also used to use white-out when we made mistakes, which was a real pain and quite messy. Most of it ended up on my hands, or if I were using carbon paper, I'd have to blow on the paper until it dried before I continued typing.

The job was going well, and I was charming to everyone that was my nature and the way I was b. It was especially important to customers who came in and got to know me. I was always in time for work, did my job as required, and helped others when they needed me. Then to my surprise, after several months had passed, I was given a raise, and I was so happy, my first office increase in salary. It may not have been very much, but it meant that I was doing a good job and deserved it.

One week I had become ill with a bad cold, and only took a day off, and asked the doctor for a note, as my boss required it. One day, that's all it was when I returned I didn't even feel well. I remember one day, particularly when I suffered my first lousy migraine headache, it hurt so much and made me feel sick to my stomach, and my vision was off. I just kept working even while this was going on because after only getting a raise, I did not want to ruin my record.

We had an Administrative Trainee who worked along with my boss. It was a woman who obviously was already in a management position, and just drifting through our branch for some hands-on training. Well, I didn't realize that I was going to be part of this. My boss came to me and told me that he and this trainee needed to speak to me, and in the basement, where we ate lunch, with the doors locked so, nobody could hear or see what was going on. All of a sudden, I was verbally abused regarding issues, which had nothing to do with me. It was making no sense, telling me that I was listening in on the teller's meeting, and other allegations, which were all lies. Why? I had no idea, and they had me in tears, I mean why would I want to listen in on a meeting that has nothing to do with me and accuse me of other terrible things that came out of nowhere. I was a victim, and they were using this as part of the training, it was not only wrong; it was done with no witnesses down there to see what took place. The games that people play do they even realize how they affect people? Or do they even care? After this, so-called, 'meeting' I was so distracted I immediately got on the phone to the Human Resources at the Head Office, to advise them of what took place. They took the matter seriously, especially after I also brought up the fact that the Administrator had a strange demeanor about him. I told them of a time I went downstairs to the basement, where the lunchroom was to get something from the stationery room, only to find him standing there in his underwear. I said that he stood there with no explanation. Before I left, the branch manager took me into his office and apologized for what had taken place during his absence, which I appreciated, but at the same time, I just wanted out.

My next position was going to be at the Head Office in Human Resources as a Stenographer. It was great to be in this building made of marble, they called it the 'Ivory Tower' and had 72 floors in total, me being on the 20th floor. The atmosphere was so much better, the people seemed more helpful, and I was able to learn quite a bit more about the Bank I wanted to work for so badly.

We frequently received job postings, and to my advantage, we would get them before any of the other departments did, so I kept my eyes peeled. This position was a much busier job, had a lot of typing and dictation into a recorder, which meant I had to use an earpiece to hear, which wasn't always easy, I have to say. While you're reading this, I'm sure it seems like I worked during medieval times, especially with today's standards. Oh, and never mind the handwritten letters and forms I was asked to type, they looked like a six-year-old had written them, and these came from higher management people, educated people who should at least know how to spell but didn't.

I would take a train to work every day as it was quite a distance from the suburbs, however, at least it was like a Via train and much more comfortable than that of the subway I had to use in the past, which I couldn't stand. I got to know people when I traveled to work as I saw them daily. One stood out in particular and ended up being quite creepy. He was a police officer and worked downtown. I honestly must say I felt this man was stalking me. He did seem harmless, and knowing he was a police officer at the time gave me some comfort when I would talk to him. While waiting for the train, it never failed; he would always seem to find me wherever I was expecting. Then he would sit with me and talk about the entire journey, which I didn't mind at first, but he became kind of flirty with me, which made me uncomfortable. Then, to find out he was married, it made me feel even more uncomfortable with the way he would speak to me, and if I tried to keep the conversation at a minimum. He was never in uniform when I saw him and kept trying to tell myself that I was safe, as he was a police officer.

Then, although I didn't know how long this had been happening, he would follow me to my office building, which was all underground from the train station, and of course, there were stores, restaurants, etc. so it wasn't like I was walking in a dark tunnel with him, but it was starting to creep me out. Once I reached my office building, he would continue to his job, but I had to ask myself, is this guy for real? Is he a police officer or just some kind of stalker?

After this went on for a while, every morning, when I got to the station, I would walk to the very end of the platform, trying very hard to avoid him. It seemed to work as far as not meeting him there for having him sit with me. However, he always seemed to catch up with me while I walked to work. I was pretty naïve, although it seemed so innocent at first, to me until it became very uncomfortable, that I had to avoid him by stopping at a store or restaurant to pick up my breakfast, hoping that he would finally get the message.

I think he finally did, but I grew very paranoid and felt I had to look over my shoulder every day on my way to work. I mean honestly, that early in the morning, having to deal with someone who seemed like a pervert was not an excellent way to start the day.

I think it triggered a memory I had as a child

when I was seven years old. I was walking home from school when I lived in England and always used to take a shortcut through one of the department stores. I remember while I was looking at something, having this older man standing behind me, pressing on me, and hearing his breathing, which scared me. When I started walking home from the department store, this older man was following me. I remember running all the way home that day. Well enough about perverts, just thinking about him gives me the shivers.

I had a few confrontations with a couple of people in my department, especially this one woman, who I didn't report to, but felt it necessary to make me feel as though I did, you know, one of these bossy types which let their positions go to their head. Well, not to start problems, I used to do whatever she asked until I was told by one of my co-workers not to be intimidated about her, as she was just a bully.

I remember meeting the Senior Vice President of our department one day, and I must say he was a handsome man and seemed very down to earth, which was nice to know that he was approachable. He would always greet not only the Management but us little people as well. Most of the executives worked on the 24th floor at what they called 'Mahogany Row,' That is what it was. Should you need to see one of them or deliver something to their secretaries, you had to sign in at the security desk before entering through these glass doors, and I must say it was stunning. The desks were all mahogany, and behind each secretary were built-in filing cabinets and cupboards all in mahogany. Then the executive offices all had mahogany furnishings, sofa, expensive paintings on their wall, and someone to serve them coffee or whatever they needed as they had a maid who worked on the floor in the closed-off kitchen.

I must say that I felt it would be my goal to become an executive assistant on Mahogany Row one day, working for one of these executives. However, the vice presidents didn't have that luxury, but did have amazing furniture, but was in an office that was accessible to other employees if need be.

The executive of our department got promoted during the time I was in that department to the President. His and the CEO's office was on the 72nd floor, surrounded by security, along with a dining room with their chefs, for the executives, their clients, and specific occasions. The first time I delivered an envelope there, I was just in awe, as I hadn't seen anything like that before.

It seemed like it would take me an eternity to ever get to that level, as the vice president secretaries became what they called a management one position, and senior vice president secretary a management two and so on. I know I had a way to go, but I always did my best when it came to my work but had a lot to learn, and I was still using a typewriter.

Several months down the road, I saw a position come up for one of the senior Management. It was a woman who I had heard a lot about, all well, as she was brilliant and going places in the Bank. It meant a grade up for me, so I thought I would apply for it, not thinking I would get it, and also not sure I could ever work for a woman. I asked for the job anyway, and it was on the 24th floor, not far from Mahogany Row, and the department was the Special Accounts Management Unit. I must admit I was nervous just applying for the position, but it would mean only an interview. I found out that I was one of the candidates for the job once I asked and got my interview. She was an influential person in the Bank, and I think that's what made me super nervous. But when it was my time to meet her, strangely enough, my appearance meant more to her than my qualifications. I mean, I qualified for the position; however, she spoke to me about what she expected from my appearance. I found that a bit strange, but tried to understand that I was representing her, and would be meeting and speaking to many customers of large corporations. One thing she especially liked was the fact that I had a British accent.

The interview went very well, she asked many questions, and I believe I may have made an impression, although after talking to her and all the expectations she had for the person who got the job was high, I did feel a little scared. However, I was pleased to hear that I got the job, yay!

On the first day, I must admit I was nervous, it was a very open concept, and I wasn't in the corner, I was out working where other managers worked even though I wasn't one. I did, however, have to work with them, which was part of my job. She explained the importance of how I answered and spoke to the customers, who called, and she liked the way I spoke and how much I would be involved with dealing with these corporate customers on the phone, knowing their files, etc. It seemed overwhelming; I won't lie, but the two other managers I worked with reported to my boss, and I was lucky that they were gentlemen in the proper sense of the word, and their sense of humor helped my days.

I knew that she would be going places because she had a significant impact on the people and the executives she worked for, so it was quite a pleasure to work as her secretary.

Well, while I worked for her, the day came. Finally, came the day of the computer. I taught myself how to use it, only after being shown how it worked. I had reports to do on this, which were 30 pages or longer, and I thought that I would never be able to do this. Well, I guess I should have had more faith in myself than I did. I taught myself how to use that computer inside and out to the point when anyone had a problem, and they would not call I.T., they would call me, who would have thought!

At times the job did feel repetitive with report after report, but some of it was fascinating reading, as these being well known large corporations, it was dealing with all the problems they were going through. It was shocking to see how many of these companies got away with thousands, if not millions of dollars. As I've stated, I also enjoyed the people I worked with, as it wasn't business all day every day, we used to joke around, so it was pretty pleasant, and I was happy working for my boss, as she was terrific. I knew that she would be going places, and I was right, she got a promotion in another area of the Bank and unfortunately could not take me, as there was an existing secretary. However, those job postings went to every department, and I came across one. The job description was work for the secretary to two vice presidents who worked in an area I had never heard of, nor did I know such a field existed. It was Mining Engineering Special Accounts. So I felt I had most of the requirements and applied for the position. To think it had already been six years that I had been in the Bank, and they went by pretty fast.

Well, I got called up for an interview; however, this was very different for me. It was an interview with both executives in the department at the same time, which was a bit intimidating. This department was on the 23rd floor, one down from Mahogany Row. It seemed crowded, the desks were all pretty close together, and I couldn't see myself having much privacy there. They both looked like professors, and they even spoke in that fashion. Unlike the job I was in, I could tell that these guys were not looking for pretty or well dressed; they wanted someone competent. This job included doing their expense accounts, including their travels to various countries, some of which I was unfamiliar. They asked if I was familiar with working on expense accounts, and of course, my answer was no, but I was willing to learn. I had one advantage if I got this position: there was another secretary there who would be able to train me. I didn't think I would get it as there were so many others qualified for that position, but it wasn't an area many would want to work for, and I was lucky that my boss put in the right word for me.

It was always nerve-wracking after applying for a position and waiting even after the interview, but I got it, yes, another yay!! I was accepted, and this would mean a promotion for me to a management one position, as this now would make me an executive secretary. Boy, it wasn't as glamorous as what I had seen on Mahogany Row. I had to learn how to convert all these different currencies to do their expense accounts after every trip they made to these faraway places, and I won't lie, it was damn hard.

Every time they took one of these business trips, I cringed, as not only did I know I would have to arrange their flights and hotels, I knew that when they returned, I would have to go through all their bills. At the same time, they were away and worked on their expense accounts, which I submitted to accounting, and these guys are not organized. The bills, given to me in a mess, and sorting through them was a challenge. There was another girl there to help me out when I had to work out the currencies. But that was not all, as their written report was unreadable. They always asked for everything as soon as possible, which put a lot of pressure on me. I mean, I was using a computer, which I had only just learned, and the reports were so dull and so very long about the mining industry the various rocks, stones, or whatever it was that they were there for and the companies who required financing. And let me tell you, as well as the bills being a mess, so were the reports and it's like they expected magic.

Did I have a life other than this? Yes, I did and was dating, but nothing ever serious, besides I was so exhausted every day I didn't even feel like going out.

Anyway, back to these 'professor's, I guess I may as well call them that, they just didn't seem to belong in the banking industry, it was so strange, no wonder I got the job, I am sure others didn't want it after seeing what is involved. One day I had this colossal report to type out, and they were always on my back asking if I had it completed. The worst thing happened, somehow the power cord under the desk became loose, which made me lose power on my computer, and I lost everything, about 35 pages, and I was in a real panic. But what could I do, I mean, I apologized, and I guess I should have backed it up much earlier when typing it but didn't and it was already after five in the evening. I had no choice but to start from scratch and type the damn thing all over again while getting frowned at and stay until completed, and no, I didn't get paid overtime. I mean that could have happened to anyone, it's not like I did it on purpose, why would I? It just caused me to double the work, and there was no choice.

These guys were not like the management team I worked with upstairs, I don't believe they knew what it was like to smile, which didn't make it the best environment to work in, but it was a step up, and I had to make it work. I guess it was time to grow up and face the world, which meant dealing with people that I had no choice but to please, as it was my job.

One night, I got together with a few people I knew from a previous job, and we went to the pub next door. That's when I found out that a popular heavy malt beer did not agree with me as it made me so sick. However, I had to try it at least and, yes, I wish I didn't.

I remember one of the girls I worked with having a Halloween party at her apartment one night, and I loved dressing up for these parties. When I got to her place the night of the party, I knocked on the door, and when opened, was decorated amazingly well, as it was pretty creepy. Not only that, but I also didn't recognize most people, who were in full costume, and nobody would say who they were, so it was pretty cool. No doubt, as the evening went on and the drinks were plenty of people started to reveal themselves, it was awesome. She had some male friends who were from the other building by her, who were all police officers join the party. Well, I was pretty surprised, not having partied with officers of the law before, and wow could they drink! During the night, I had no idea what was going on in the bathroom, with a couple of them with a few girls, but they were pretty noisy, no not the girls, these officers. I know that we were all looking from the balcony as two of the officers had their police motorcycles out, and had the girls sitting at the back of each of them and just speeding up and down the road. They did finally come upstairs, but I thought to myself, who would have known that officers of the law would party that way out of hand. Thank god nobody was injured, but my eyes watched taking all this in as it was all new to me. Just as well,

I was staying over at my co-worker's place overnight because there was no way I would be getting home after all the drinking we did that night. However, I do remember that I paid for it the next day when I made my way home and unfortunately had to take the subway with a major hangover. Every time the tube jerked, it made me feel so ill. When I got to my station, I ran as fast as I could to the nearest washroom, threw my overnight bag on the floor, and I will spare you the rest as it was unpleasant, and I had the worst headache ever. It was a new experience under my belt, and alcohol was the last thing on my mind.

Well, I'm glad all that happened on a Friday night and I had the weekend to recuperate. Come Monday, and it was back to work and those long reports I had to type. It seemed that the two executives I was working for traveled so much. I dreaded it because I knew that once they returned, I'd be dealing with some new currency when it came time to do their expense accounts for each place visited.

Reading this, you must be thinking, this woman got bored with her jobs rather quickly, which is partially true. However, I wanted to be in a position in which I got something out of and enjoyed. It was too bad when the woman I worked for moved to a new job and couldn't go with her because I enjoyed working with her. She taught me a lot not, only about the situation but about life.

I always kept my eyes open on those job postings, in case anything appealed to me, and I had been in this position with these mining engineers for over a year now and felt that it was enough. I wasn't getting any satisfaction from the job, and they didn't give me any praise, which would have been nice. It just started to get boring, the same old reports, the same complicated expense accounts for these guys. And as I had stated earlier, the surroundings were so tight and also really dark, which made me pretty miserable.

Finally, I saw something that seemed appealing to me. It was for an executive secretary for a marketing/training executive, and it was in another building, not in the Ivory Tower, which was ok with me as it wasn't far from there. Besides, I didn't even know if I was going to get the job or not yet. You guessed it; I applied for the position, and now it would mean waiting because there were many candidates.

I didn't realize how every position I got in this Bank affected me in so many different ways. I was such a 'virgin' in the workplace; everything I dealt with was new. In such a short time, I had already learned how to be taken advantage of by others, become a victim to bullies, overcome my fear of learning something new, and teach myself new things. After all, I never went to college or university after high school, so it was all hands-on training and life experiences.

A couple of weeks had passed, and I figured, as I had not heard that it wasn't right. Then all of a sudden, I had a call telling me that I had an interview. For some reason, I became extremely nervous, whether it was because it was going to be out of my comfort zone, which I had become used to in the ivory tower, and would have to go to an entirely different building. Or the fact that it was a department I knew nothing about, marketing. The only marketing I had ever known was what I learned in high school, as one of my courses was marketing. Also, I had heard about this executive from other people who knew of him. He had high expectations, in what I have no idea. I know that he had just joined that department itself, so being new together made me feel a little better.

I appreciated and always remembered that after working for a woman, she helped me realize how important my appearance and telephone manner was for any person I worked for, as I represented them and the company. She always complimented me, and knowing the importance of my appearance after her talk stayed with me forever. With this in mind, I went and purchased a new dress for my interview.

I hadn't changed very much in appearance over the years, and was still very petite, with long hair down to my waist. I remember it being a sunny day in summer the day of the interview; my dress was form-fitting but classy, and I headed to the other building making sure I was ahead of schedule for the meeting. When I got there I had to go to the 6th floor, and it was not a tall building, but it was quite a lovely area and walking distance from where I was at present. When I got to the location, it wasn't a massive area like the head office, where I was at today. One of the girls who worked there asked me to take a seat as he was presently in a meeting, so sat there tapping my fingernails together with nerves as I had no idea, apart from what was on the job description said, to know what to expect. He then called me into his office and told me to take a seat. He was an older man, well dressed, and got right to it. Surprisingly the first words out of his mouth were, "well, don't you look lovely." What did that mean? Did it imply he liked my dress, my hair, what exactly? I didn't know how to respond and just thanked him rather awkwardly.

He asked if I would like some coffee, and then he proceeded with his questions. He asked me if I was married, which never really came up in my past interviews, and I wasn't sure what that had to do with the job itself. I told him, no, and he went on to say that it was good that I wasn't. Again, I thought, why would he say something like that, and when were we going to get to the actual interview. He had this strange smile on his face, and of course, trying to be polite, I smiled back. I tried to think nothing of it, as this job was essential to me as there was the hope of promotion within the department, and he finally started to ask me work-related questions.

He asked about my computer skills, which at this point, I was doing rather well, asked if I knew shorthand (for those of you who don't know what that is, as I don't know if it even exists anymore) it is a symbolic writing method rather than longhand. It means that you would be able to take dictation very fast, which I did not have experience at and was something my mother grew up doing in all her jobs, years ago. So here I was thinking, well that's strike one against me; however, he didn't seem to bring that up as being a problem. The department seemed pretty interesting, as it would mean I would get to learn how to do page layouts for advertising or training within the Bank. That was appealing to me, although training would be within the department. He also traveled, however, not as much as the mining engineers I worked for at present. Even though I hadn't officially got the position yet, he showed me around, showed me where I would be sitting which was right outside his glass-encased office, which meant he could see me at all times, something that was new to me, and I wasn't sure how I felt about that. The desk itself had some as it was kind of enclosed. The staff seemed pleasant enough. The interview seemed to last forever in my mind, but it was actually about half an hour. He shook my hand and told me that it was a pleasure to meet me and hear back from human resources if I got the position within the next week.

I left the interview feeling good but didn't want to get excited about it if I didn't get the position. So now I had to walk back to the ivory tower back to the mining engineers. To my surprise, I could not believe that they told me that they didn't think I would get that position because of my experience. I was thinking to myself, thanks a lot!! It was almost as though they wished that I did not get the job. They brought my mood down immediately, and I mean, who likes that, and it made me feel like I wasn't worth anything, the nerve of them!!

The following week dragged, and because it did and I had heard nothing made me feel like the guys I worked for at that time, maybe right, maybe I wasn't qualified to get the position. That afternoon to my surprise, I had found out that I got the job and would be starting the following week. I sure you must know what I wanted to tell the men I was working for at present, but I wouldn't lower myself to say anything to them. They congratulated me in a kind of oppressive manner, but I kind of expected that from them. I didn't need them to be happy for me, as it felt good and I was ready to celebrate with some friends at the end of the week.

When I began packing up a box with all my stuff, it felt terrific. It was a fresh start for me away from this building, at least for now. I made sure to thank everyone I worked within my department, as there were people who helped me learn a lot during my time there.

Finally, Monday came, and for once, I was happy that it did. I was excited to get to my new job at the new location. It felt a bit strange taking the elevator to the 6th floor in a building with only ten levels, but I had a good feeling once I stepped out on the floor that was now to be where I would be working. I'm glad that my new boss allowed me time to adjust to my modern desk to make it feel like it was mine. Then the phone rang, and for a minute I had to think to myself, what department is this? And I hesitated, thank goodness someone answered it for me, and it was good because I believe I would have drawn a blank.

Once I settled in, I felt I didn't have time to breathe and take it all in before being handed my first assignment. That meant getting used to someone else's handwriting, and thank goodness it wasn't pigeon scratch as I had seen in the past, it was almost legible. I didn't realize that, as my boss was the Vice President, Marketing/Training, which meant he was in charge of the entire department in this building, so it made me feel great that I was working for the 'head guy.' The work was pretty impressive; a lot of it did have to do with training within the Bank and advertising so much better than rocks and stones (giggle). So my first day seemed like a success, and I left there feeling content. I was still able to take the train home, as the distance wasn't that far from my old job. The downtown district contained all four major bank head office skyscrapers, all within the same vicinity. This area often used during the production of a movie or T.V. series, is something I found exciting after I saw them shooting a scene one lunch hour. So before I continue telling you about the new job, let me backtrack a little.

During my time of working downtown and watching that movie production, I thought it was pretty amazing to watch. I remember one day during my lunch hour while watching this movie production, one of the P.A.'s came up to me and asked if I was one of the extras, I politely told them no (wishing I was, as it all looked so cool), and made sure I wasn't in their way. It made me curious about how I would become an extra for a movie, so I looked into it, found an agent, did my headshots as required, and went from there. They knew I had a job, but they got jobs all the time at different times of the day, whether it was very late at night, really early in the morning or weekends, so it was possible to get involved. I told them I was willing to ask for vacation time if it meant I could get a job as an extra for any upcoming movies, T.V. series, or whatever they may have.

Well, I managed to get some work in several

movies, all of which I kept a log on for myself to look back on. Some of the calls involved hundreds of people, and those were the worst because you had to check-in, have your make up done if a costume was required that was another line-up, and the worst was lunchtime, as they would order catering for us, but when there was a large amount of us, it sucked.

So yes, I was an extra in several well-known movies, some T.V. series and I remember one documentary in particular, which was about hurricanes, tornados and bad weather in general. There weren't many extras required, which was great, and the timing was right to work with my regular job. The production took place in a warehouse. I was supposed to be a passenger on a plane. However, it was a quarter of an aircraft, but the inside looked all very real. We took the scene that was supposed to be during a tornado. When I think back about it, I still laugh to this day. We had our seatbelts on, and when "action," they had this partial plane moving around as if we were in a storm. They had a massive fan because, in the scene, it was supposed to have caused damage to the plane, and there were all kinds of things thrown in front of that fan so that it would look realistic, us being the panicked passengers getting hit with all these flying items. Once they said, "cut," the fan was shut off, and we would repeat the scene, we went through this several times until they got it right. We couldn't say a word; however, we could mime as though we were speaking, crying, or panicking. It was hilarious because all of us involved would get our hair all messed up, with things all over this piece of the plane, and when it was time to do a retake, we all had to have our hair done again, everything had to look normal in the plane, which meant the crew had to clean up each time they did a retake. However, they managed to get in 3 or 4 takes, and this would only be a little scene in this documentary, but it took a few hours to make. I remember when I received a call for a car commercial going to air in the U.S., which was a late Friday night right through to the next morning.

I also remember an infomercial, which they did on the weekend at a home they rented. It was for this iron, and we did have to say a few lines. There were two of us for that, and most of these were for the U.S. only. I also remember doing a scene for a futuristic movie where they had one of these broad stairs on wheels, we were in costume, and had to go up these stairs and down the other side, and that was it. With the use of the green screen was us stepping into a spaceship. I thought that was very cool. However, I didn't see that particular movie once it came out. However, I did see myself in a few others, which were pretty cool, and that minute would have taken an entire day to produce. It was pretty fascinating, and I'm happy that I experienced as much as I did in that industry. It was getting to be a bit too much with my regular job, so after doing it for a couple of years, I decided to stop as you didn't make a lot of money as an extra at all, it was just a fun experience. I did, however, make more money for the commercials and infomercials. So yes, that is just a little glance into my life as a movie extra.

Well, getting back to my new job, I guess I got a little off track there, sorry about that. The job was going well, and I was beginning to feel quite comfortable, then my boss called me in and said that he needed me to take some dictation, I reminded him that I didn't do shorthand and he told me that's fine just make it longhand. Well, that was a challenge, but somehow it worked. It was a busy department, but an interesting one, especially learning how to set up pages for presentations, not on the computer but using all the marketing tools the department had. It seemed different from my other positions, and I seemed to receive a lot more respect from members of the department, something I had never really experienced. Maybe because I was working for the head of the department, I don't know.

I found it strange when I started getting calls for him from two women who always asked for him, and it did not seem business-related from what I could tell. What was even stranger, although they were both two different people, they had the same first name. Sometimes when I'd let him know one of them was on the line, he'd roll his eyes and tell me to say he's busy. I knew he was a married man, so that made me a little suspicious of him.

I had met his wife several times when she would meet him for lunch; she seemed a fundamental old fashioned type of lady who didn't look his kind, that's if he even had a variety. I couldn't tell either of their ages, and it's not something you bring up in conversation. When she did come in, she was very focused on him and him alone, while he didn't seem very loving to her, and I thought to myself, please, I don't need this kind of drama in my job. Was he having affairs with these women who called? Well, from sources within the department, that seemed to be the case. I had just got this job, and I thought I had better stop with the gossip and get on with it, however, all this drama did play a part in it.

I remember him asking me to plan a vacation for them, and he told me where and when and just said to get the best accommodations, fly first class, etc. I didn't seem like money made a difference to him; he felt the more he paid, the better vacation he was going to have. I guess that could be true, but I would think who you would make a huge difference. So I did as he asked and it came to over $15,000.00 for the both of them for a week. Wow! I couldn't even imagine having a vacation like that book for me. However, I was a little jealous. At this point in my life, I hadn't traveled much at all. I thought to myself, and I guess this is how he keeps his wife happy while he continues to have his affairs. Personally, any money in the world couldn't make me happy if I knew that the person I was with was doing this to me. I wonder if she had any idea.

When I think back to my interview for this job, he was a little flirty with me, but I thought nothing of it then. Having a glass partition, as part of his office, which faced my desk suddenly, became an invasion of my privacy, as I must admit, I always felt his eyes on me, which made me quite uncomfortable. Why would he even want to look at me, I didn't consider myself anything special, and there is no way I would ever want to get involved with a married man. Suddenly this became a concern for me because I didn't want to have to face that decision and just hoped he kept his life to himself.

Sometimes when I would take him coffee into his office, he would just start chatting and tell me to sit down. Then he decided to say to me that the two women who called, both names being Jane, were lady friends of his, saying this with a smirk on his face and letting me the one with the African American accent was a woman he'd known for quite a while, and the other not that long. Still, he didn't want either of them knowing the other. I have no idea why he confided in me, and I honestly wish he hadn't told me, as I must admit, I lost some respect for him that day. It was bad enough being told by a fellow worker, but having the nerve to say to me that face to face, was I to expect that keeping his secrets was now part of my job? It was even worse when he went to meet them during work hours, and I had to make excuses for him, also when his wife called.

I have to be honest; the familiarity he had with me at this point seemed somewhat premature. He didn't know what kind of person I was, and to be frank, his daily gestures towards me began to feel uncomfortable. Knowing the type of man he was, I tried very hard to continue working with him on a professional basis, but things seemed to be the opposite. It was a real relief when his vacation with his wife came around as his behavior was beginning to creep me out. I dreaded when he came back, not that I didn't like the man. I felt what he was doing was wrong, and I didn't want to fall prey to him.

Then one day he received a call from head office that he had been given a promotion to Senior Vice-President, I thought I would be going with him, but assumed wrong. There were many applicants, and my boss would interview them from his fishbowl of an office. He would throw me a smirk every once in a while, as though he was trying to make me jealous.

After several interviews, which seemed as though he were just interviewing these women to torture me, he told me that I would be going with him to his new job. Well, no doubt, I was happy; after all, this was my career, and it meant a promotion and a salary increase for me, and I professionally thanked him.

Yes!! Finally, I was going to be working at the 'Ivory Tower' Head Office, on 'Mahogany Row,' something I had been waiting for a long time.

There was a lot of preparation before moving there, packing, shredding, etc. Once we moved, glass doors, which were locked, now protected me, and only those allowed were allowed in. With security watching over all of us who worked in the mahogany row, it felt like a safe environment. I had a beautiful mahogany large desk with a security button hidden for any emergencies (apparently, it was a requirement in this department). Behind my desk were floor to ceiling mahogany filing cabinets, cupboards, and a fantastic computer. The best part was that he was in an enclosed office. I was not on display for his enjoyment, which was a relief.

I did notice that working on that floor, the 24th floor of a 72 story building, meant it was time to buy some new clothes, as the dress code was quite different, and had some class to it, besides it was an excellent reason for me to buy new clothes. Of course, my boss complimented me, but in a way, I wished he didn't, and it wasn't appropriate, in my opinion. Comments like "that look very sexy on you," "that really emphasizes your breasts" and "maybe you could get something a little shorter," were just a few of the comments which I just laughed and tried to ignore but it wasn't easy, and I felt very uncomfortable. I mean I had bought some beautiful skirt suits, dresses, most were form-fitted because I was slim and they looked cute, pencil skirts and nice silk blouses. They were most of my new wardrobe for my new job.

My boss, whose name I have not mentioned yet, only because it makes me shudder to think of him, so I will continue to refer to him just as "my boss." He would find any reason to call me into his office, his eyes always looking as though he were undressing me, so I would do whatever I had to and quickly get back to work at my desk.

In the mornings and afternoons, all the executives in that department and their assistants, including me, were brought coffee or tea and cookies, by a lovely woman, Jan, who worked in a closed small kitchen area that she maintained. If my boss wanted another cup of tea, he asked me many times if I could get it for him as he was particular in the kind of tea he drank, and of course, it was another excuse to get me to come to his office.

One particular day I went in there to get his teacup and saucer, and dropped the napkin on the floor, as I went to pick it up he also went and made me jump as I thought he was about to touch my leg as he brushed against my thigh. He asked me, "what's wrong; I'm not going to attack you?" Let's just say I just wanted to hurry up and get out of there.

At times if he set up a meeting in one of the conferences on the floor, I was responsible for ordering refreshments and food for the attendees. He would ask me to bring it in, rather than have Jan bring it in for them, as that was her job. I found out the reason for that was to show me off as though I was some kind of pet. After the meeting, he would brag about what some of the executives would say about me telling me they said he had one of the best-dressed assistants. As if that would matter to me, I would forever get smirks and comments from these executives and managers who attended these meetings. He would make me come into these meetings, whether it was for one thing or the other. But because of my innocence, I didn't realize that what they were saying was not appropriate and, most of the time, tried to accept their comments as a compliment or just laugh and ignore the comment made.

Back in those days, women never really spoke about sexual harassment, so you had to learn how to deal with it, which wasn't easy. It did make me wonder how they could get away with this kind of behavior. I did feel seduced by a predator, and he just happened to be my boss.

I made many travel arrangements for him, as this new job involved many business trips, especially to the U.S. When he returned, I would have to claim his expenses. There were many slips he gave me, which were for personal things, and he would write something to validate that it was part of the business trip. It always made me feel very suspicious of him and who knew what he did while he was away from where nobody, including his wife, could check.

I honestly believed that he was entertaining women during the trips, as that seemed to be his thing.

One trip, in particular, included the President of the company and other executives to Brazil for an unusually large conference, which seemed somewhat overboard for what it was. When he returned from that conference and gave me all the expenses to claim, I could not believe what came out of his mouth.

He told me while they were there, they had a blast, drank, and had some kind of Mardi Gras during their trip. He spoke of the women in their skimpy outfits the dancing they did, which included them joining. I was wondering to myself, what kind of conference was this exactly? He proceeded to tell me; the executives got together to hire a prostitute for the President of the company at his request. Seriously?? Even I knew that was so very wrong. After I heard all the details, I was so happy I didn't have to hear or speak about it anymore because it was all very secretive and I spoke of it to nobody else.

As I worked for this man, I became very suspicious of him; he had come on to me several times, done inappropriate things in private to me, and in front of his peers, that I felt a need to find out more about who he was. So the detective in me came out of hiding.

I knew I had to be careful because this was my boss, and I had my job at risk if I was going to look into this man's past to find out who he is. I kept this to myself and didn't tell a soul, but knew there was more to him, because of his cheating, lies, and conniving ways. So, where did I begin? Back in those days, Google didn't exist to find out people's past, but I had access to all of his personal histories, which I felt during his business trips I would be able to look into further.

I was fascinated by a strange way to see his past positions, jobs he had elsewhere, and countries he lived in for a short time. He was German, that he made quite clear to everyone, not that it should have made a difference to the type of man he was. From what I could see, he had worked many kinds of jobs, but what puzzled me was a position he had in Germany, which seemed rather short before him coming to Canada, so that was the place to begin. His name seemed different when he lived there, and I just thought maybe he was using the English version but wasn't sure.

Who would have thought how much you could find out about a person with the right resources? Now that I knew the name he went by in Germany, and surprisingly through the library, I could go back years, especially with the use of a Microfiche, something I had neither knowledge of nor how to use it. I got the help I needed, and I believe I became obsessed with this in my free time because I knew I was going to find something on this man and was determined to do so.

During the time I was in the office, I did my job, avoided his advancements as much as possible, and tried my best to ignore comments from the other executives because I have no idea what lies he had told them with his filthy mouth. I guess at this time in my life, I didn't have much of one, so this was the ideal time to do some digging, and so it began.

Having his past information was huge because I was able to look back at his youth in Germany, and it wasn't right. He had been arrested several times for theft, breaking, and assault. In particular, one stood out to me, where he had been arrested for but not convicted. Apparently, in the small town he lived in, he had sexually assaulted a 13-year-old girl, but due to lack of evidence, the case went cold. I knew it! I just knew that there was something about him that seemed evil as he looked as though he was not all, but there was more.

A year after that, there had been another assault, but this was a brutal one. It was a young girl of 15 who went missing, and my boss, who I will now call 'the criminal,' was involved with her.

She was an apparent acquaintance of his, he knew her from school and was seen with her at a park the day she went missing by a witness. They took him for questioning; as a minor with a record, however, treated as lightly as his previous crimes. He was 18 years old when this took place, so he went back many years, and it was around that time that he had come overseas to live in Canada by himself, not with family.

I knew someone who was in the judicial system in Canada, and a friend of mine was working as an undercover cop, new at the job, but I knew these people would be able to help me look in the right places I needed to find.

I went back to this missing girl and followed up on it to find out that she was raped violently and left to die. My boss, was nowhere to be found for further questioning, they had mentioned that there was a search out for him, but how he left Germany on his own at such a young age without being questioned and arrested I don't understand, I could only think that somehow he had changed his name, I mean he was involved with criminals there before all this, I'm sure it must have been pretty easy to get out before they found this poor young girl.

I had to question myself, was I getting carried away and accusing him of something I don't know he did, even though the German newspaper had named him a suspect, but he left the country.

The witness who had seen him with this girl had said that he had her by the hand and seemed to be forcing her to walk with him. Nobody saw him after that day, not at school, nowhere. So what was I to think? With my friends' help in law enforcement, I was getting more help finding things out now, as all I had before was the microfiche in the library.

My friends wanted to know why I was looking into this guy. I didn't want to let them know I was working for him and just looking into his background, not yet, anyway, so told them that it was a sensitive issue, to please trust me and help me all they could and that one day I hope to say to them everything. Their main concern was that I was in no danger, and as far as I know, apart from being seduced by my boss, I couldn't say anything at this point until I found out he was the same man that left Germany after that violent crime. Also, I did not want to take advantage of my friends working in law enforcement because this wasn't anything to do with something from the present, and I wasn't in any danger, not yet anyway.

I do believe I was handling myself rather well, considering the past my boss had. I began to react when he would make the advancements towards me, which he consistently did in the privacy of his office, especially. Something came over me which took away the fear I had of him, and I was learning day by day how to deal with this man, this predator who knew my every move, watched just about everything I did and seemed to keep me on a pedestal as 'his,' well so he thought. I was in a job I had been waiting a long time to get, in the department I always dreamed of, and this man was not going to scare me away that easily, and I was going to make sure of that.

He never spoke of his wife, considering he shared other personal information, and I had no interest. So one day, I thought I would ask him how she was, as a general type of question. To my surprise, he said, "she's gone for a girls vacation" to the Hamptons. My response to that was, "Wow, now that's unusual, you have always gone together on vacation since I worked for you." He just chuckled to himself and said, "Well, this was long overdue." Long overdue? What should I read into that? I mean she was not the type to have friends, he said that some time ago. She was his wife, and that was it, and the last time I saw her, she seemed to be under his control. I could not imagine her going to the Hampton's without him, and it seemed rather strange to me, but I thought I'd better leave this entire conversation alone, although I was concerned for some reason.

So in my head, I thought that this seemed rather dangerous leaving this man, this predator alone at his home, for who knows how long, as he never specified how long she was going to be away. Some days, it was difficult to concentrate on what I was doing, because half of me was doing my job, and the other wanted to play detective. I had been given some great advice and tools by my friends in law enforcement and intended to further my investigations of this man because I knew he was not just a predator; he was a murderer. I was going to do everything I possibly could to prove this and hopefully have him pay for his actions. I mean if he did that so many years ago in Germany, who knows what criminal activity he's done here. I knew this task at hand was not going to be an easy one, but as I said earlier, I had become obsessed with this and was determined to find out more. I felt this was part of my life's journey; I know it was not part of my life's plan, as I had achieved what I wanted to do as far as my job went. It was as though a force unknown was telling me to find out everything I could, and I knew I had to be very careful.

I'm sure you must be thinking to yourself, 'do you not have a life?' Well, I did, but this became a big part of it. I began reading books about serial killers, their behavior, backgrounds, and what possibly makes them kill. I felt I needed to dig deep so that I knew what I was facing.

I started working early and into the late nights, as that was the time I could do my research. And finally, computers were getting more advanced, just in time, as for sure I was going to need this as the central part of my resources. I had the key to this man's desk and drawers in his office, and during my late nights, I would search for anything I found that may look unusual. For example, he used to keep a journal, which I wanted to go through but had to be careful, as I know he would notice if anything in his office were not in its place. I saw on his calendar there was a big red circle around the date when his wife was supposed to have gone to the Hamptons, so I continued to look through this journal to see if I could find out why she was there and was she there with friends? As I flipped through the pages, I came across one entry: "thank god she's out of the picture, she has no family here to ask any questions, but I must come up with an excuse should anyone ask." I asked myself, who was 'she,' and was he referring to his wife? I suddenly got goosebumps running up and down my arms, as my mind traveled to some dark places.

I read a few other entries, one said, "Really enjoyed watching that young girl, such purity, untouched, I must follow her again." Again my mind began thinking the worst. He knew how to seduce a woman, he did it to me, was he preying on young girls now? And where? It was disturbing to read some of the entries; they would go in-depth into his fantasies, which weren't helpful. I then thought to myself, no wonder he seduced me, from the first day he interviewed me, he could see right through me. I was very innocent, and he took full advantage of me. So who was this young girl he was speaking of in his journal, and was she going to be in any danger?

I know what I was doing was wrong in some respects, I was going through someone's journal, but at the same time, I knew it might help me find out the bad things he may be doing. Each morning I would come into work, avoid eye contact with him as much as possible, and try to get on with my work. This one particular afternoon, he said he would be leaving early, and if I wanted to, I could leave as well. Perfect!! I knew what I was going to do.

He parked his car underground, in a different area where mine was parked, but I decided it was time to follow him. We took the elevator together; I wished him a good evening and proceeded to my car. I watched as he pulled out and slowly followed him through the underground parking and out onto the streets. It was raining, which didn't make the visibility very good at all, and I didn't like driving downtown, but only started to do so, once I decided to find out who my boss was and what he was doing in his spare time.

As I drove, the thought ran through my mind, that who would even give him a second glance. He wasn't a handsome man, not in my eyes anyway, was it the way he seduced, the way he would tell you how beautiful you were and tell you what every woman wants to hear? Anyway, I had to stop thinking and start concentrating on the road. I thought we'd be driving a while, when suddenly he made a sharp turn right, not far from a private high school, where he had been before, seemed to be familiar with the area and knew where he wanted to park. Not wanting to be seen, I quickly pulled into a parking spot and waited to see what his next move was going to be.

To my astonishment, I saw that he had his window rolled down and was calling someone over. I couldn't hear, not only was it raining, but also I was parked away from him. I then saw this young girl with long black hair in a uniform walk towards his car. She bent down, and they were obviously talking, and she looked like she was about 14 or 15 years old, in my head I was hoping she was not going to step into his car, and then it happened. She shook her head in the motion of agreeing to what he was saying to her and got into his car.

Oh my god, what was I to do? I had no idea if he knew this girl was related to her; it's not like I could just go up to his car and drag her out. My hands were tied, and I felt so helpless because all I could do was watch. But I was not going to drive away, I had to follow them, and the rain was coming down harder, which made it even harder to see, that I lost sight of his car. I felt panic because I didn't know where he was taking her, I didn't know what to do, and I still didn't know if she were maybe a niece or some family member. I felt the need to drive to his home to at least see that they did not go anywhere else, but when I got there from the outside it looked like nobody was home and he had a garage, so I had no idea if the car was parked in there or not. I had no choice but to leave and go home, which was not easy for me to do, not knowing who she was and where they were.

By the time I drove home, I was tired, confused, and did not feel like doing anything to keep my mind off what I had witnessed. I tried to go to bed early but could not sleep knowing that a young girl could be in danger. I woke up in the middle of the night and thought it would be a good idea to start making notes, and that is what I did, wrote down everything I had seen the night before.

The next morning was a Friday, and being in as early as I usually was, I expected to see him there, but he did not come into the office until noon. That was most unusual, and I knew he had no meetings that morning, so where could he have been. I asked if he was ok, and he said he was fine, in an abrupt tone of voice. I brought in his usual cup of tea, my hand trembling slightly and noticing that his left hand in a bandage. I asked if he had hurt himself, and he just said, "I was having problems with one of my tires and cut my hand while trying to fix it, no big deal."

Ok, well, that could be true, I guess, and maybe

that girl was some kind of a relative? I didn't know what to think at this point because the injury being something to do with his tire seemed to make sense. So I thought I'd just make random conversation and asked if he heard from his wife and was having a good time. His response was short and said, yes, she was having fun. After that, I thought I'd try and keep to myself most of the day, but it was hard to concentrate on my work. Thank god, the weekend was here!

There was no need for me to stay late, so I left at the usual time, which was earlier than him this time. I was happy the week was over, but I had to admit that I could not get that girl out of my head.

I had no plans for the weekend and thought I would give my active brain a bit of a rest. I relaxed, did some cooking, and wore my comfy clothes laid on the sofa and watched some T.V.

While watching a show, an amber alert came over the T.V., and my heartfelt like it stopped for a moment, as I saw the photo was of a missing 14-year-old girl with long black hair, last seen wearing a school uniform. I could not believe my eyes, and looking at her photo on the screen, I could see that she was a beautiful young girl, and I could only think that she was full of innocence. What had he done? What do I do? I was scared because I could point the finger at my boss, the predator, saying he took her. I didn't know the details; I am not sure if he just gave her a ride because of the rain, but come on, seriously? If he did that even at that age, he would have put on the charm and seduced her. What was I saying? I was so shocked and confused. I had no idea what to think. I knew he was home alone, but I didn't see him take her there, I didn't even know if he was there last night. I could only think the worst at this point because he spoke of a girl like her in his journal.

I felt like calling my friends who had helped me that worked in law enforcement, however, if I told them I followed him, was that the right thing to have done? What would they think of me, and have I gone too far? Many questions were going through my head, and when I decided to call them, all I said was, "Hey, I saw the amber alert on T.V. last night, that was awful. Any idea where she is or any kind of leads?" I was surprised that they didn't ask me why all the interest; however, they did mention that someone saw her get into this black car, other than that there was nothing. I knew that eventually, I would tell them, but now was not the time, even though I knew I could trust them to investigate my boss more than I could, I had to make sure. I mean, as far as they were concerned, I was an Executive Assistant, a friend who asked them to trust her when they last helped me dig deeper into his life with the resources they had at the time.

Meanwhile, going through my head I thought

to myself, maybe I am in the wrong profession, I so wanted to help find this girl, I wanted to get my boss arrested for the girl he allegedly killed in Germany, all this going on whatever information I had obtained over time. With him having changed his name, marrying and becoming an executive who would ever believe me? I was beginning to feel like an accomplice because I wasn't bringing it to the police's attention after following him the night before, so I had better tread rather gently from now on.

Weeks passed by, and nothing was on the news about that young girl so, what was I to think? Had I made all this up in my head? I had to think about everything that brought me to this conclusion. I thought if he had done anything to her, they would have found her by now. On top of that, he never spoke of his wife returning from her time at the Hamptons, which seemed strange. I didn't know if I should even ask him at this point. He had been quite quiet these past few weeks, which was unusual, as he always had something to say. I thought I would leave the questioning for now and carry on as healthy as I could be, considering everything that had happened. It wasn't easy because I spoke to nobody about what I thought and what I had done to this point, and it was going to stay that way until I felt the time was right.

It was December, and it felt quite festive everywhere with the lights and Christmas trees. Our department looked beautiful. For a while there, I forgot about everything and enjoyed my surroundings. Without thinking, I asked my boss if he and his wife had plans for the holidays, well, that was bad timing. He told me that she had gone missing from the time she was at the Hamptons. I expressed my concerns and said that I was so sorry to hear that and asked if her friends knew anything. His response to that was an abrupt "No." I daren't ask if there was an investigation because he bluntly closed the subject in question. There was something wrong here, and no doubt, I was not going to find anything out because I was the only person he had told that she went on this vacation is these friends of hers, which I knew did not exist.

Should I even think the worst? Did he do something to his wife? I mean, I didn't make any arrangements for her to go up to the Hamptons, and I've always booked their vacation plans. It was driving me crazy not to confide in anyone about everything that had happened to this point, so I decided to continue to journal from the time the young girl had gone missing. It was a way for me to release everything on my mind without anyone knowing. I had a few friends, but none that I wanted to confide in at this point. Being Christmas, I went out for drinks and dinner with a few of them, something I don't often do as I am a bit of a loner, and that suits me fine, especially when I'm playing detective.

Weeks passed, the New Year had come, and all the beautiful festive decorations were coming down. I never heard any more about that poor young girl, and as far as my bosses wife, he treated it like she was dead, not missing. He had kept to himself quite a bit for a few weeks, I didn't know if it was because he was sad that his wife went missing, or because of the guilt, he felt for the losses related to him. Then all of a sudden, he was like Jekyll and Hyde, from not talking to getting a bit too familiar with me once again. Did he not know that this behavior of his was so old to me by now? Not because he was worse than ever, and I did not appreciate the things he said to me. For the first time since I worked for him, I spoke up and said, "I don't appreciate how you're speaking to me," I could not believe his response when he said, "It's time for you to grow up little girl," which he followed with a wicked smirk and just walked away from me. My jaw just about dropped, only when I picked up the courage to let him know how I felt, he put me where he wanted me back in my place.

By now, there were ways of bringing up sexual harassment charges against individuals primarily in the workplace, but that would be my word against his. Because this law was reasonably new, I didn't think I'd win the battle, and would likely lose my job, which I did not want. So once again had to deal with him in my way, which could be overwhelming.

His wife went missing just before the young girl had me wanting to put pieces together once again. I had to find out what happened to them, but how? He had the nerve to tell me that many times during his business trips, he picks up hookers. Really? As if I wanted to know, and I wonder what he does with them or if they go missing, I shudder to think about it.

It was the New Year, and the workflow became quite busy, and I knew I had to focus on my job and get my head out of detective mode. I'm glad because it meant he was working, and I didn't have to put up with any nonsense. The department was changing, getting more substantial, and there the entire infrastructure was going to be quite different. It didn't mean a job change or moving from where we were thank goodness, but it did mean more interaction with other people besides my boss, which was a good thing, especially right at this time when I was preoccupying my mind with everything else but work. All this change meant training in various areas taking courses at our training facility, which also had a hotel in it (which belonged to our company) for those in classes for more than a week and found it hard to travel back and forth. The trouble with having staff under the same roof after a day of courses was like watching university frat parties going on, but that was not my problem. Not that I thought it was a bad thing, but because, as I've stated, I am a bit of a loner.

I had to attend a management course there for a week, which with all the changes happening, and I didn't mind at all. It was quite refreshing. I was also away from our office, which I think was something I needed at this time. Many people got together after a day or leaning for dinner and drinks, but I excused myself. However, I did go to the bar (within the training facility) as I just felt like having a drink, alone with my thoughts. One of the guys, Jim, who worked within our department, took a course at the same time, and just happened to come by the bar while I was there. I turned and smiled and said, "Hey Jim, so how's the battle going with the courses?" He replied," pretty good, how about you? We don't see much of you when you're working on the mahogany row. However, we hear a lot about you." I asked him what he meant about understanding a lot about me, and he told me that obviously, my boss does not hide the fact that he brags about me, (like I were his property), and not about my work, of course, it was all sexual talk behind my back. I told Jim not to believe everything he hears and said to him that it's not easy working for him and that I am learning how to handle him. Jim continued asking me if I was alright and that there was something I could do. In return, I told Jim that I appreciated his concern; however, I was in a difficult situation with my boss, and it took me a long time to get to mahogany row. I did also mention, just to make it clear to him that I loved my job, but what comes with it isn't something I expected, but I will not be out of a position I worked hard to get. I didn't want Jim to know what I was dealing with and that my boss had tried to seduce me when I first started working for him, as much as I would have loved to have told someone about what I had been through, I had to tread lightly and represent myself as the professional person that I was.

After having a friendly chat with Jim, I excused myself and told him I was calling it a night. I went up to my hotel room, changed, and turned on the T.V. About an hour later my phone rang, and of all people, it was my boss. He said, "So how's the course going, are you learning anything new?" I replied, "It's going well, and yes, I'm learning a lot and meeting many of the people I don't see daily." Then, of course, his true colors began to show, as here I thought we were having a normal conversation, although I didn't know it was normal for him to be calling my room. He proceeded to say, "so have you met any men, and chuckled, has anyone hit on you yet? You know if I was there, we could have had dinner drinks, and then who knows what could have happened." At this point, I was just disgusted and told him, "First of all nobody has hit on me that's not what I'm here for, and I don't appreciate you saying that. Secondly what you are saying to me is very inappropriate, and why are you even bringing all this up, why are you phoning me at my hotel room? It's not work-related." He said, "I'm checking on my girl, well you have a goodnight, and I hope nobody is there with you." Just as I was about to respond, he hung up, leaving me with that disgusting thought in mind.

Here I thought I was having a great week with my course, and here he dares to say these things to me by calling my room? It seems I cannot escape him even by being at the training facility, I guess that's what a predator does, and I did not like it one bit. I finally got to sleep, and it was hard to concentrate the next day on my course after having all that said to me last night, but it was the last day of the course, and then the weekend would be ahead, something to look forward to hopefully.

Once I got home after the course, I unpacked, and I just wanted to do some more research about this man. I thought I had put it aside, but that didn't last long, and with him speaking to the way he did, it made it so much more important to continue and let the detective in me come out once again. I tried to keep up with the latest news hoping that there was still hope for that young girl who went missing, supposedly, as far as his wife going missing, it's like he just shut the book on that, but why? It was all very suspicious, and especially after I saw that young girl get in his car, I could only think the worst. I only wish the rain didn't come down so hard that night so that I could have continued to follow his car. I already had plans to check out his journal, which is locked in his desk, unless he has hidden it elsewhere. I know I booked him for a business trip for the Monday coming up and that he would be away for a couple of days in Chicago, which would allow me to see if there have been any more entries. And speaking about journaling, I added what he said to me over the phone to my journal, as I felt it necessary, and if I ever do get to prove that this man is a psychotic murderer, I need to keep as many notes as possible about things he has done or said to me.

The weekend went by quickly, and Monday was here, it seemed to go by fast. I'm so glad that I don't have to face him today, especially after what he said to me while I was away taking a course, and he has not changed. I mean, why would he? How does a man like this become a senior executive of a company? So many things have been going through my head, including not being arrested when he came to this country from Germany, changing his name in the process. From what I read about criminals and murders, they know how to get around just about anything, which is pretty scary, as they also seem like ordinary everyday people.

I couldn't wait to look for his journal, and thank goodness he hadn't moved it. So I began reading some of the entries..." the feeling I get is an instant high, "I'm in control, and my sexual needs have are met."..."There didn't seem to be much of a struggle, as she was quite petite, but touching her body, although cold and still got me aroused once again, and the feeling of finding another got me excited". " It was like going to a toy store, picking out the one you really would like to play with, and then throw it aside." "Having my hands around that thin, soft neck and squeezing gave me such sexual pleasure that I came."

I sat back in the chair in shock after reading the details of what seemed to be the young girl who went missing that he was speaking about; I mean, who else could it have been?. I jumped as there was a knock on his office door, "where's your boss today, is there any way of arranging a meeting," it was one of the other executives, I responded, "he's in Chicago for a couple of days; however, I can let him know when he returns that you'd like to meet with him." After having that knock on the door, I took a deep breath, scared the hell out of me. I proceeded to read some more of the entries, which made me sick to my stomach. I knew that he had plans of finding yet another girl, and where was the other one he lured into his car that rainy day when I followed him? That's one thing he never seems to mention in his entries.

I know I should have been showing this evidence to the police. Still, the fact that I followed this man, knew he had the 14-year-old, and did nothing and now was reading his journal, that could make me an accomplice, and it wasn't my intention to hide all this, I just didn't have any solid proof, not yet anyway. If I showed the journal to the police, they might have just read into it much differently. I felt the need to tell my two friends who had helped me out when I first started to find information on my boss, the two friends I had in law enforcement, but one had moved to the U.S., and I lost contact with the other. Damn it; I should have told them why I was doing all this back then, he could have been charged by now.

But what was this fascination I had with this predator, was it because of how easily he was able to seduce me? Did I want to see what made it so easy for him to find his prey? I knew one thing for sure. I didn't help the 14-year-old, and if only I were able to follow them further, I might have known where he took her. Were my fascination and curiosity getting the better of me? I hope not; I know that I was a victim of his. However, it would have been difficult for him to make me vanish as he did his wife and this poor young girl. People knew that I worked for him; they knew his unusual behavior toward me; if he did anything to me, it would be far too obvious. Anyway, I had work to do, so I locked up the journal for now, but I was concerned about wanting another girl.

The day went by quite fast, as I did my work, but I could think of what he had written in his journal in the back of my mind.

Well, no doubt the two days he was in Chicago went by rather fast, and once again, I had to face him in the office. I can only imagine what he'd do while he was away, and that would not only be work-related but would involve hookers. Thank goodness there was other Management there with him for the same meeting. Otherwise, he would just stray and who knows if there would be another victim. After reading his journal, he thrived on the feeling he would get while hurting another person; it was sexually arousing. When he went into his office, he suddenly came out and asked me, "did someone need something from my desk?' The hair on my arms stood up, and I could only think, oh my god, did I not lock the desk? I responded, "No, um, I was just looking for an appointment book." He was not happy and made it known. Just by the way he spoke to me, it was harsh. I apologized for forgetting to lock it up and told him that his office was closed while he was away, so nobody else would have gone through his desk. He told me to make sure that didn't happen again. How stupid I was to leave it open was a careless move on my part, and if I wanted to hide what I knew about him, this must never happen again.

I tried to get back on track with work and told

him that one of the executives requested a meeting with him and carried on with my day, avoiding eye contact with him, in case he could see right through me. I felt so scared wondering what was going through his mind, knowing that I had a key to his desk and could have found just about anything he had hidden. I tried to make conversation asking him how the meeting was in Chicago, bringing him his tea, and trying to get his mind off the fact that I left his desk unlocked. Later in the afternoon, he told me he would have to leave early, and as usual, he said to me if I wanted to go home I could do so.

He was mad, and I knew he was leaving early to prey on someone, and I was ready to follow him once again. I know it was risky and to see how angry he was today, I also knew it wasn't safe should he see me. One of the other executive assistants who sat not far from me, Anna, asked me, "So what's wrong with him today? He seems angry about something." I told her that he was having one of his bad days. But this was the first time he brought attention to himself in the office and not in the right way. Before leaving, he had asked me to make reservations for him at a local restaurant, so did. I wished him a good night, and he went out of the office with a pretty stern look on his face. The reservation was for two, and I knew it wasn't work-related, so I became suspicious, and this would be an excellent opportunity for me to be at a location where I could see him and even if he did see me, I was in a public place.

I wasted no time, packed my things together, and headed out. Because the restaurant was within walking distance, I had no reason to take my car. The restaurant he went to had several areas; part of which you needed reservations and the other you could just walk in. Once I got there, I made sure to get a seat at the bar, making sure I had my boss in clear sight. I managed to see where he was sitting and just as I thought he was with a young woman, someone I had never seen before. I watched as he put on his charm to impress her, if she only knew what his intentions were or if there was some way I could warn her of him, but my hands were tied, and it was out of my control. I was at the bar and was able to blend it with everyone; however, my eyes focused on them, and although I wasn't sitting facing them I sat at the side of the bar where I had a view of them in the large mirror on the wall, and just had to look to my right slightly so that I had a clear picture.

Of course, it came to mind, why would a beautiful young girl be there with him? She didn't look like a prostitute but could have been an escort. I really couldn't tell, as strange as it seemed she seemed to be enjoying his company. It is being a predator he knew how to manipulate a woman, to make her feel like she was extra special and would behave very gentleman-like with her, knowing that it would likely impress her even more. I knew this because he had done this to me in the past. I didn't want him to see me, and it had already been over two hours, and then I saw him get up and leave with this young woman.

I quickly paid my bill, and once I came out of the bar had lost sight of them. I feared the worst, however, could not do anything, so made my way to get to my car in the underground parking of where we worked. As I was getting ready to leave, to my surprise I saw his car still sitting in the parking lot, so it left me wondering if this meant he was going to take out his anger on the woman he was with and began to think the worst, however, there was nothing I could do or was there?

When I got home, I phoned my friend of many years who had been in law enforcement and was also transferred to the US, as did my other friend. I just wanted to ask him the question that had been playing on my mind all this time. I asked him, "Jim if you felt someone you knew was a serial killer, what would you do?" Jim sounded surprised and said, "are you speaking of an actual person or is this a general question?" I felt I needed to tell him my suspicions especially as he was going to be leaving soon, so finally shared everything with him. He was shocked to hear all this but even more shocked that I had been following the suspect and not bringing it to anyone's attention. I told Jim that I was afraid to bring it to the police's attention because I didn't really have proof and felt they might consider me an accomplice because I had not come to them sooner. Jim said; "you're stepping on thin ice you do realize that? You should have at least told me, and now that you have kept this to yourself without any proof, you can't very well go to the police and just accuse your boss of these crimes, and even if you do, yes, of course, it's going to make you a suspect, because of everything you know. Please just leave this alone, I can check him on our system, but if as you said he changed his name when he came here from Germany, it's going to be pretty difficult." I knew I should not have brought this up to anyone, but I was bursting at this point and thought if at least he did a background check on my boss maybe something may come up. Jim told me he would get back to me, but was concerned about my safety, and I understood that. We had been friends for many years, and he along with my other friends who were now in the US had helped me with advice in the past so I felt I could trust him and told him I would wait for him to call me back once he did the background check.

It was just after 9:00 pm, and the phone rang, it was Jim. He said; "I ran a background check on him and apart from him reporting his wife missing, he had a clean record." I thanked Jim for doing this for me and for listening and showing his concern for me. He told me to be careful because he wasn't going to be around for long and told me he was worried about me. I told him not to be, that I have been cautious about making sure my boss doesn't know I have been investigating him on my own and should I get any proof, that I would bring it up to the police. But in my mind, I knew that I was just saying this to him to put his mind at ease. I know for some strange reason I had developed a peculiar fascination about my boss, the serial killer. I wished Jim all the best and told him that I would miss him but asked that we keep in touch.

Thank goodness it was the weekend because I wanted to look into taking a night course on Criminology. I know it covered Criminal Behavior but also included Forensic and Criminal Psychology, which was extremely interesting. While I looked into the courses available, I saw that they offered online courses, which was perfect as it means I could work in the comfort of my own home, especially now that I had a computer. I thought to myself, this was huge for me as I never thought I had it in me to go on to college, but there was something I was so interested in, I registered right away. It was a big step for me, and I felt I wanted to understand my boss, 'the Predator', the 'Serial Killer', both of which to me, seemed that same. If I was going to continue investigating, I needed to educate myself about the behaviour of a criminal so that I would know how to deal with him daily, knowing what he is capable of at the same time making sure I am safe. I knew it would be fascinating and was excited to get the books and start the course, which would be the following week.

For the rest of the weekend, I relaxed, did some reading, and focused on myself until the news came on the television. As soon as I saw them post this photo of a young woman on the screen, I raised the volume to hear what they were saying about her. Was the woman who was in a restaurant with my boss? My heart started to race, and for some reason, a feeling of panic hit me. They announced that this woman had been found strangled to death in an underground parking lot downtown. I knew that it had to be the same parking lot where I parked my car. I listened to some more only to hear that she had been sexually assaulted as well. Another young life, taken, and it had to be him, the man I worked or. I started to feel like his accomplice because I was doing nothing to bring him to the attention of the police. Why was I not doing anything? And now I was going to take a course to study him? I began to wonder what was wrong with me. I know those parking lots had cameras everywhere, did they not see who did it? From what they were saying there were no suspects at this time, but why? How could that be missed? Was he that smart that he knew exactly where to do his crime to avoid the cameras? I was not looking forward to seeing him at work on Monday. My actions were all feeling too much like a guilty pleasure.

Monday came and here I was back at the office to face a different type of reality as it has been feeling like I have been living two lives, the Executive Assistant and the Investigator of Crimes. It gets difficult to concentrate at times because my mind wanders. I mean after I am working for the Predator, it's hard not to let my mind wander, especially after the recent murder of the young girl I saw with him on Friday just last week. How the hell do I prove him to be a killer? I do not feel prepared to, at least not at this time.

His mood seemed much better today than on Friday when he left early, the same day I forgot to lock his drawer, which he kept in his secret journal. I wonder if he suspects that I may have read what was in there and was waiting for the right moment to face me with it? That then made me wonder what he might do to me, and I had to get that out of my head and concentrate on my work. Strangely when I was in his office at one point during the day he asked me; "so how was your weekend?" I told him that it was excellent and very relaxing. I didn't want to mention to him that I had registered for a course, especially the one I had enrolled. So I quickly asked him how his weekend was, and which a bizarre grin and a creepy voice said; "it was very satisfying." I didn't want to ask him anymore after that as it made me very uncomfortable.

Sometimes I would catch myself just staring at my computer daydreaming of what one of his victims must have gone through. Why the hell would I think of that, it was sick! Was I trying to put myself in his or the victim's shoes? When I caught myself doing this, I would get up and take a walk as this was consuming my mind, maybe my life, as this had been going on for the several years I had been working for him. And I had done nothing but followed him, read the entries in his journal, knowing that he had killed and was going to do it again, but I had no intentions of quitting my job or applying for another. I knew my fascination with him and what he had done was not right, yet I wasn't doing anything to stop how I felt, I mean I was even going to be taking this course I registered for only to find out more about how a mind like his works and why.

That afternoon I went for lunch to the restaurant where he had taken that young girl. I just wanted to have one drink and sit by myself and go over what happened that night, almost like I tried to put myself in her shoes and imagine what he may have been saying to her, and then I would think of where they went after that. I had ordered some food, but daydreaming once again it had got cold, and I had barely eaten anything. I looked at my watch and realized

I had been there for an hour and a half, so quickly paid my bill and walked briskly back to the office, thank goodness he wasn't one to question why I was late. While I was out I had picked up a newspaper as it had a photo of the young girl who was found dead in the parking lot, which I found out was our parking lot, but put the newspaper facedown as I didn't want him to see what I had been reading. When I came in this morning, I had seen the yellow crime scene tape boarding off quite a bit of an area down there, not an area near where I park, and it was way off in a corner, once I saw the location, I could see that it may not have been visible on the security cameras. It was an eerie feeling but at the same time got my curiosity juices flowing, I know how confusing that sounds, but those feelings seemed to exist, and there was nothing I could do about it, or maybe I didn't want to do anything about it.

This week I began my online course, and I felt the rush as soon as I started, as it was what I was hoping it would be. Maybe now I can learn how a serial killer thinks, put myself in their shoes, feel what they feel and try to understand why they do what they do. I know it sounds like I am becoming more obsessed with this entire matter, but I couldn't help myself, and I don't think it was a bad thing at all. What I hope to get out of this course is that crucial information I need to go forward to the police and tell them about my boss, at the moment I couldn't, as they would question why I hadn't come forward from the beginning. I am beginning to feel like his accomplice so had to make sure I got all the facts I required before even thinking of going to the police. I do believe I wanted to feel I had control over him, that I could, at any time have him put away.

So a week had gone by, I went to work, as usual, things seemed pretty reasonable, well as healthy as they could be, I guess. The course was exciting, and the assignments were rewarding as I was getting what I wanted from them. The tasks were quite easy to complete and wondered if it was because I felt I was already in the head of a murderer. And that wasn't a bad thing as the course put you in that position to be able to learn how they think, why they do the crimes, and how they try to cover up their crimes. I was beginning to believe I was in the wrong profession thinking that I should have studied in law enforcement; however, at the time my goal was to be reminded of the Executive Assistant in the Ivory Tower, and I succeeded. Who would have thought that my life would take a sudden turn to become so involved in crimes? And I knew in my heart that I was wrong for not speaking out sooner to the authorities, but I wasn't going to give up and was determined to get what I had to report my boss, the serial killer, to the police.

I knew that one of the first things I had to do was to try and get my hands on his journal; hopefully, he had no clue that I had read it. He had a meeting, which was out of the building for a few hours, so I knew this would be my opportunity to get what I needed. Once he had left, I took the key to his desk, left his office door slightly open, and searched for the journal, which I thank god I found. I know that I needed some proof, and this was where I would begin. It was great that as the years passed computers and electronics, in general, had improved so much and so quickly. I now had a cell phone, which had a camera, and had that with me in the office. I flipped to the pages I had once come across and took photos of the pages I really felt would be relevant. It made me sick to my stomach when I reread those entries, but it was crucial to have this. Once I took the photos, I made sure to place the journal exactly where it was, and this time I did not forget to lock the desk. I put my phone away, after making sure I had the photos saved, and returned to my office to continue with my work. I'm sure you must be thinking of how I was able to concentrate on my regular job with all this crime surrounding me, to be honest; I don't know how I did.

It was time to go home, and my boss wasn't back from the meeting, so I packed up and left to go home, as I knew I had an assignment due for my course and wanted to work on that at home. I noticed that I was beginning to seclude myself, as this became part of my daily life, and I barely ever went out with friends anymore. Once I got home, I had a nice hot bath, changed and got to work on my assignment, when suddenly my cell phone rang. I was shocked when I found that it was my boss, how did he even know my number, it's not something I shared very often at all, and I had no idea how he got it and didn't want to ask at this point. However, I did tell him that I was surprised that it was him on the phone. Still, before I could continue, he said to me that he would not be in the office for the next couple of days and told me that there was a vital envelope he wanted me to bring to his home, which I found strange, I would typically send something like that via courier. I agreed that I would, and said that I would call him before leaving the office tomorrow. His voice seemed rather anxious, loud and not too friendly, and I barely had the chance to say bye as he hung up rather quickly after that. Now I began worrying what this was all about, and my mind began to wander. I had to come to my senses and continue my assignment, which was due, however, that night I did not get any sleep. I was scared and wondered if I was going to be his next victim.

The next morning I woke up as usual and made my way to work with that laying heavy on my mind. To my surprise, the security guard on our floor advised me that I had a delivery. Nobody was around as it was still pretty early, so I decided to take the package and try to get this over and done with and took a cab, which would be paid by the company, rather than driving my car there, as I was sure I'd be back by late morning.

He lived an hour and a half away from the city. During the entire drive, my thoughts were all over the place, and I wondered why this package was so important? Why did I have to deliver it personally? I kept thinking back to those women he had seduced and killed, but really could not get myself to bring it to the attention of the police. Again, would I be looked at as an accomplice because I had watched every move and done nothing about it? Was it just that I was somewhat curious in a slightly weird way? I hadn't seen him commit the actual murders, but all the proof I had witnessed, led him to be the murderer and his past, which I studied, proved he had all the characteristics of a killer. Where would I even begin to bring this up with the police? I would be his stalker if anything, but would the police even understand? I just couldn't take risks, of course, I felt remorse for all those poor women, but I would not have been able to stop what happened to them, unfortunately.

We were almost at his home, according to the driver. It was pretty secluded, and I know he owned a couple of properties. However, this is the one I know he lives on a day-to-day basis. My eyes opened wide as I glanced around to see if there was any other home insight. Although we did pass several homes on the way, we had to drive up a country road, which seemed rather narrow; the fields were rather wild and disregarded. We were finally here. It was a large home, it looked rather old, and there were no other homes in sight. As I was getting out, the driver asked me if he should wait, but I knew this wouldn't just be a drop-off, it's never that easy with my boss. So I told the driver that it was ok, and thanked him for the asking, as he did look somewhat concerned.

I tried to ring the bell, which didn't seem to work, so banged on this large, robust door several times, until I heard him say; "ok, ok I'm coming", in an abrupt manner. While I waited for him to get to the door, I looked at my surroundings, which seemed desolate. As he opened the door and invited me in, the place seemed nice inside, but he had very conservative tastes, and a lot of the furniture was dark wood, some vintage pieces, from what I could see.

He asked me to come and take a seat in his living room, which I did and sat on this rather cold leather sofa and handed him the package. I was going to ask him what was the urgency, but I should know better than to do that after his call the night before. He put the package on the coffee table and stared at me for a minute, which seemed like an eternity because he did not say a word but just looked pure evil. I could feel goosebumps come up on my skin, and it wasn't because I was cold, I became overcome with fear. He had a fist up by his mouth as though he was preventing himself from saying anything. I didn't know what to do, I mean, what does one do when you sit across from someone who stares you down and says nothing? I stared at the floor then at him, I looked at the walls, then again at him.

Finally, he put his hand down from his face and avoided mentioning the package and asked me if I would like a drink. I told him water would be fine. When he brought the water and I was reluctant to take a sip as who knows if he had drugged it, but I didn't have a choice, I asked for water so took a sip. He then proceeded to ask me; "do you know why I asked you to bring this package to me?" I said, "no, but you sounded rather frantic, so I assumed it was something important, urgent and maybe personal." I could feel my heart beating so fast, not knowing what he was to say next. Was I overly paranoid? Was I making something out of nothing? All these questions were going through my head when he finally told me.

A smirk came across his face, and he proceeded to say; "No this is nothing really, I just needed to get you here so decided this was a way to do it without making it overly obvious to anyone." He then opened the package, and all that was in it was an old newspaper, it looked ancient. He then laid the paper on the table. I asked, "What do you mean, I don't understand, besides why would you not want to make it obvious that I was delivering this to you?" He chuckled not in a fun way but pure evil. "You see this newspaper?" he said, "it's German and ancient, and I do believe you know why I am telling you this." I proceeded to tell him that I had no idea what he was talking about, that I just did as he asked, but I felt I knew what was coming and it scared me.

He proceeded to tell me; "I have made you come here to make you aware that I know what you have been doing behind my back, your research if that's what you want to call it. I have had people follow you, just as you have followed me, for years now, do you think I'm stupid?" I had no words; literally, I listened in shock, and because I do believe he was going to face me with every act of murder he had done from a teenager in Germany. He was cunning in the way he managed to get me to his secluded home, without my car, not having a clue where I was, I had no choice but to sit there and continue listening in fear.

He then said, "Why so much interest in me? Did I succeed in seducing you that you became so interested in every detail of my past?" As I was about to respond, he continued, "What made you so interested in me, was it the loss of my wife? But then, of course, you know that her disappearance was related to me, didn't you? I responded; "I...I was just concerned, you said you came from Germany and I just wanted to see where you were from, your background, I didn't expect to come across any records of you as a teenager and the crime you committed." He said, "crime? Was that your interest? Let me tell you, young lady, and one does not dig so deep into someone's past to find out everything you did for no reason. I am surprised that since you found out so many details about me, you haven't come forward to the authorities, or have you? I responded, "No, I have not, why would I? I can't prove anything, as I said I was just curious about your past. I didn't know you were responsible for killing that girl in Germany, I mean, why would I want to go to the police, what if I was wrong?"

I decided to stop talking, as I may have just been letting him know how much more I knew about him at this point. I mean he already brought up his responsibility for his wife missing. I have to admit that although I was fearful, I couldn't wait to hear more admissions from him, but why was I sadistic? Why wasn't I told that I should get back to work to try and get out of there? Something just kept me there, and it was him and everything he was about to tell me.

I sat there as though I was a child listening to a fairy tale. He told me every dirty detail about what he did to that girl in Germany and then proceeded to tell me how he planned the disappearance of his wife but did not indicate too much about that, not yet anyway. He then told me; "Don't think you're going anywhere, because you're not!" I then said, "but why, I have not told anyone about you or what you may and may not have done, for that reason that I had no proof and for all I know I could have made this all up in my head. There is no need to keep me here; people will look for me." His plan to get me there worked, but I had no idea it would come to this. He spoke angrily, but at the same time now and then an evil smirk would appear on his face.

He said, "whatever your little scheme or game was with me, it is over, do you hear? Your curiosity excites me, and yes, I will share every detail with you." He then told me after leaving Germany; he couldn't believe how easy it was for him to change his name and make up a new past. He expressed the sexual pleasure he got from killing the girl in Germany, and that it was a feeling he craved as the years went on. He said his wife's disappearance was effortless, then pointed out to a barn on his land, telling me; "You see over there, you could say that's my playground, I have taken not only my wife there; after I drained the life out of her very slowly the way she deserved it. Oh no, and she was not the first to be taken there, and she will not be the last."

I had no words, of course, I was scared, but yet curious, that's one of the feelings I have not been able to understand about myself. I could try and escape from the home, but where would I go? There wasn't anyone for miles; even the road leading to his house was all his private land. He showed me the barn from a window in his living room, which was in the distance, hearing him call it his playground could only mean one thing and I did not want to become a victim there, so rather than showing my fear, I expressed my interest, which may have caught him by surprise, but I had to do this. I do believe it was the only way I was going to stay alive at this point. He asked me if I would like something to drink, I asked if he had tea or coffee, and then went to his kitchen. It was the perfect time for me to leave, I mean it wasn't that easy, it would have been different if he had left the car keys somewhere in sight, but of course, he didn't. As my eyes searched, of course, I didn't dare get up and walk around, I heard him say; "Don't think about leaving, the doors are locked", he chuckled "of course I have a security system and made sure to close all of them as you came in."

The feeling of the locked doors caused me to feel extremely anxious, something I didn't want him to see, as I tried to play it pretty cool with him, especially at this point. Shortly after that, he came in with a cup of coffee for me, and nothing for himself. I thought to myself, what if he's put something in this? Is that it, am I going to be another victim in his "playground"? So asked him, "Well, aren't you going to join me with a drink?" He replied, "I guess

I could", and poured himself a bourbon. Well, what was I to do? He could have put something in the water I drank earlier, and he didn't, so I proceeded to sip on the coffee while he sat back in a chair, legs crossed and just stared at me again with an evil smirk on his face and sipped on his drink. I had no words, and he said nothing at this point. It didn't take very long when I began feeling strange, and my eyes started to blur. I was wrong, he put something in that coffee, and I passed out.

When I came to, my right ankle was attached to a long chain, and I was lying on a dirty mattress. It was dark outside and not very bright wherever I was at this time. I could barely see my surroundings and could hear the rustling of leaves and the wind blowing. I was hoping that I was not in the barn, which had become; I know it was referred to as the "playground", and where the hell was he. I got up from this mattress that God only knows what or who had been on, and I felt very light-headed still. I saw that he left me a small flashlight, how damn kind of him and a bottle of water, which still had the seal on it, which I drank rather quickly. He was nowhere in sight so I turned the flashlight on so that I could see my surroundings a little better.

It was not a small barn, so I took my time and made sure of where I was stepping because I did not trust what he may have set up in there for me. I yelled out for him, but of course, there was just silence along with the wind and creaking of this barn. I now felt terrified because he had gone beyond what I thought he would have done after having me come to his home. I have become a victim, something I knew could be a possibility because of my curiosity and everything I had done trying to find out what he was up to, but I couldn't believe it. I had been so careful up until now, and I could only imagine what may be in store for me, after all, he was a serial killer. I kept mumbling to myself, stupid, stupid, why would I allow myself to become his prey? Look where I am now, and the fear grew stronger, as I slowly walked around this barn.

He had taken my shoes, in case I was able to get out of that chain, to prevent me from running. The chain was long enough for me to walk around quite a bit, but I was scared of what I might find. There was a large white freezer on the other side of where I was, but I couldn't quite get to it, and maybe it was just as well, as I don't think I was ready to see what my fate may become. I felt a chill up my spine, especially after he had told me his not only was his wife in here but there were others. Please don't let me die in here; I kept thinking to myself. I had to stay somehow track of what day it was, of course, I would not know the time, as I wasn't wearing a watch, but I did not want to lose track of my days I felt I was going to have ahead of me. It was Friday when I came to his home, and that meant he was most likely going to be around. There was nowhere really to sit or lay down apart from that mattress I woke up on, and I think I became freezing due to the shock of being here. There was an old blanket that smelled disguising, but I needed to cover myself up and try to relax as much as possible because there was nothing I could do at this point but think.

As I lay down, a thought began to run through my mind about what he said about his wife and others being in here. Where did he put them? The freezer couldn't be a possibility for maybe two people, I was trying to recall some of the case studies I covered in my course to get into his head. Many serial killers used freezers; they also buried them, burnt them or disposed of the bodies in the most horrendous ways possible. I couldn't believe this was real, I wanted to wake up and have it all be a dream, but no this was very real. Then I thought to myself; people will be looking for me, my car in the underground parking lot at work. They would, of course, need to question him of my whereabouts, and others who may have seen me.

I think I was trying to make myself feel better to believe that everything would fall in place and be ok, and they would find me. In reality, nobody saw me that day at work except for the guard on our floor. Even the cameras in the underground parking lot would show that I was nowhere near my car. Nobody knew I had a package to deliver to his home; he wasn't even in the office, so nobody would know where I was. Then I began to work myself into a panic because nobody would know where I went, how I got there. I was going to become a 'missing person'. How could I be so stupid? Why didn't I tell the guard at work where I was going? And I should have just driven my car. He also thought about this instead, telling me not to use my car to drive there, have me leave so early when nobody was there for me to understand where I was going. I guess while all this was going through my head, I fell asleep.

The next morning I was shocked when he was standing over me telling me to get up. There was some light coming in through some parts of the barn, and as he woke me up I put my hand over my eyes as the sun was shining right in them, and I wanted to make sure it was he and not someone else. I asked him "why are you doing this to me?" He said, "well, you're the one that was so curious about me, and now you're going to know everything you need to know and more." While he spoke, he handed me some cookies and coffee. I found that strange as I thought he would not give a damn about feeding me, so what is his plan for me? I told him I had to go to the bathroom, so he unlocked the chain and walked me to what seemed like an outhouse, only in the barn. He let me go in and held the chain while I went to the bathroom. There was no soap to even wash my hands with and just a rag to wipe them on. He gradually walked me back to where I was and told me that we had to talk; he even brought in a stool for him to sit on.

I said to him, "people are going to see I'm missing, and you do know they are going to question you?" He responded, "I'm not worried about that, people go missing every day, do you think you're something special? You do realize that when people go missing, the cases go cold rather quickly, and besides, they won't even know you're missing until Monday when I show up for work, and you don't." I then thought the worst; he's going to kill me for sure if he's speaking about going to work and me not being there. What scared me was his knowledge of some cases going cold. I mean his wife's case eventually did; however, that was over an extended time, as he used to keep saying she stays at their place in the Hamptons. When I think back about that, I remember that the police did a massive search for her, including nearby rivers, and when there was no sign of her, the case did become cold. Unfortunately, for the girls, who went missing, I did not hear much, apart from what I read in the papers. It's surprising how many lost people are just that unless they are children, there is not a lot of effort put into others. I mean there is only so much they can do, I guess. The cases I worked on in my course were of a variety, but they were cases which were solved, well most of them.

He said; "listen, I have plans for you, you interest me because of your curiosity, but you will remain here until I am ready to change that. I will be going to work, the police will question me, but remember I wasn't there for a couple of days, so there is not much I can tell them." He said that with that smirk on his face. I didn't want to respond, I didn't want to carry on this conversation, and all I asked him for was some warmer blankets and asked him if I needed to go to the bathroom while he was not here where I would go. He threw a bucket at me with a roll of toilet paper; I guess I was lucky I got any at all but felt he was treating me like an animal, I mean why would he treat me any differently? I did ask him why he was leaving me in the barn, and he said; "I felt you needed to get a feel for where the others are, you were curious after all." He had a lock on this barn, and as he left me there, I knew that we were in the middle of nowhere and that I couldn't yell because nobody would ever hear me. I was now just left here to sit and think. I have always thought of myself as a healthy person, but at that point, I broke down and cried as it all became too real to me because it was. This time it wasn't me playing detective I was the victim, and I will remain that way until he decides to do whatever it is he has planned.

The sun was shining into the barn, which made it feel warmer, as we were in spring. I grabbed the chain and began walking around again, looking for any tools, anything which I could use to bang on this chain. Still, he thought of everything and never left any means out for me to find, after all, he's not entirely stupid, I guess. I walked around wondering where the others were or was he just saying that to scare me even more? Would I not smell the bodies if they were here? Well, after taking my course, we didn't concentrate on the smell of a dead body in a particular place, but I did know if the body was deep enough, there should be no smell. I believe having these thoughts run through my mind was strange considering I was now a victim, but that was just it, that's what brought me here in the first place, was the curiosity of it all, of him, the "Serial Killer". And what am I doing, thinking of how one would dispose of a body, what's wrong with me? If I wasn't as curious as I was, I could be far worse, trauma-tized by this entire ordeal, but strangely I wasn't. Yes, I cried, it was scary, thoughts go through your mind when you are amongst dead people, and you have no idea where. But I knew what he was for years now, and I had done nothing, why? Because I needed to see more, it just didn't make any sense, was I as sick as him?

I found little sticks on the ground and because using them as a pen on the dirt floors, to occupy myself, like a bored child. All of a sudden, I heard him open the lock of the door. He proceeded to tell me; "As you are aware, there is nobody around for miles. So I have decided to bring you to the house, you will remain in your chains, but I will allow you to join me for lunch." In my head, I was thinking, is he serious? It doesn't make any sense to me, and I just didn't know what game he was playing. It's not like he felt sorry for me, that was quite clear, but I think because I more or less kept my composure and not scream every time he showed his face. As he undid the chain from where it was secured, however still attached to my ankle, he led me out of the barn in my bare feet back into his home. He then said, "Don't think of taking your chains and trying to run out of here, first of all, you'd never make it out the door, and besides I have set the alarm to lock all the doors once again. You will sit here eat lunch with me, and I do not want a conversation, however, after lunch, I will then share some of my very private collection of photos of my work which I'm sure will satisfy your curiosity somewhat." What private collection of photos was he talking about, pictures of his work? It then dawned on me that his work could only mean one thing. He was going to share photos of what he did to the women he killed. All this brought me to the conclusion that I could never see myself ever leaving here alive.

He had me sitting there in the chair in the kitchen where he could keep an eye on me as if I could run anywhere without a long chain attached to my ankle. While he prepared whatever he was getting for me to eat, I asked him, "are you going to allow me to at least clean myself up?" He responded, "you wash when I say, you do, and you will follow every direction I tell you, whenever I ask you to do something do you understand?" I nodded my head agreeing to what he said. I mean what else could I do it I couldn't very well tell him no I want to clean up right now as if he would let me do that. He wasn't messing around. He wasn't polite and had me there for a specific reason which I still didn't know, but I was still his victim, and I had to do as he said. He then called me over to the kitchen sink and told me I could wash my hands. He then had me sit back down and brought over a glass of milk and a sandwich of some kind and when he wasn't looking I had a peek what was inside the sandwich because I didn't trust him at this point. I sat there in silence and ate the lunch and drank the milk while he told me that the photos he would be showing me were something of a trophy to him. He was a sick bastard, but I had to question myself if I was any better? I could have saved several of his victims by turning him in, but I didn't. I mean after all the studying I have done on him and all the spying I may be looked at as an accomplice. I couldn't take that chance although I know it was wrong of me and I should have brought his behaviour to the attention of the police. I still didn't understand the curiosity I had of him as a serial killer, I know he was my boss, and if I spoke up to the police, I have no idea what could have happened to me, and in that respect, I was very selfish. But to be honest, I can't explain the fascination with him that I had or should I even call it that. Am I as sick as he is? I mean I've gone as far as taking courses, not so much for the legal part of them but more for the details of the crimes involved in the case studies. I know it might sound strange, but I feel like a serial killer has seduced me, and it's not in a sexual way if that's possible. While I studied him, it created a particular attraction towards him and what he was doing. But look where I have ended up, this wasn't supposed to happen. What kind of person am I? I'm scared, but I'm not terrified because I'm curious about what he's going to show me, maybe something I've been waiting to see for a long time.

As I finished my lunch, there was silence; however, when he saw that I was done he grabbed hold of the chains and when I asked where we were going, I was told that his decision to show me the photos, was on a much larger scale and he felt I would appreciate them more. He then took me to what looked like his theatre, sat me down and proceeded to throw the chains on the floor. I guess this was something he did have planned; however, that wasn't something I was expecting at all. He turned the lights off and asked me if I was ready. I mean was I supposed to say no; because he wouldn't have listened anyway, but I had no idea what I was about to see.

He abruptly told me to pay attention, and that's when everything I thought he had become a reality. It began with his wife, who was actually at the Hamptons at their cottage, it showed him surprising her, she seemed happy, at least that's what it looked like while watching the video. If then showed him kissing his wife, which led to them being on the bed and slowly, his hands worked up to her neck. He began to strangle her, and I do believe that she thought he was playful until his hands got tighter around her neck, and I could see her struggling. I had never seen anyone die but to see it done in this fashion is unexplainable cause he kept squeezing and squeezing until all the life from her had gone and she lay there looking so peaceful, but to kill his wife was his intention and he succeeded. It then showed him going towards what was the camera. I guess it was a spy camera because it is something that she would not have seen and he recorded the entire thing. I had to turn my head and look away, and he forced me back to looking at the screen and told me that there was much more to come. What I did notice is that this particular cottage was secluded for miles just as his house was, obviously if I were to get into his head I would say it was exceptionally well-planned years ahead of time.

The video didn't end there as it showed him

turning on the video in the bedroom of the cottage rolling out plastic and then a white sheet, which he placed on her, then rolled her up in it. I saw him turn the camera off and then back on again, but this time he was what seemed like some kind of a barn, which seemed very much the same idea as his home, coincidence? I have no idea it just seemed well planned. I did not turn my head away during this time as I was curious about what he was going to do; next, I don't know why as it should have made me sick to my stomach when I saw him strangle her to death, but it couldn't just have ended there. And I was staring at the screen. He told me not to turn away because the best is yet to come. The excitement came over his voice as he told me this as though it was going to be some kind of fantastic surprise almost like it was a show and I guess it was a show in his head and I was going to be forced to watch it whether I wanted to or not. It seems like this barn was well stocked and organized. There were tools on one side that were a bench on the other they were mops and brooms, and there was a chainsaw. His Face once again came near the camera as he adjusted it to an angle that he intended to record. I then watched as he unwrapped his wife onto the floor, and I dreaded what was going to come next.

I turned my head away again, and his hands forcefully made me face to screen. What I saw next or shocking as he took the chainsaw, he looked up at the camera with an evil smirk on his face and proceeded to saw her arms off with such ease. I told him I felt sick to my stomach. Still, he just said to me that this is what I wanted to know. He wanted to see this because I was so interested in him and told me I was going to watch this whether I liked it or not and handed me a bucket to throw up in if I had to because he did not want his theatre messed up. My eyes welled up with tears, and the tears rolled down my face as I watched him dismember her body piece by piece. He had garbage bags beside the body where he placed the parts of her, as I watched this, I felt the need to throw up. So my suspicions were correct the entire time, but I had no idea he went to this length. Once he had put all her parts in the garbage bags, he approached the camera, and as he wiped his head blood covered his face and the camera was shut off. I don't know if I could ever remove the image from my mind, but this is where my curiosity had taken me, and I still question myself as to why.

The chains were heavy that it prevented me from getting up, and he stood in front of the screen as though he were giving a presentation. He then said to me, "Well was it everything you wanted to see and more?" He said as he smirked and seemed so pleased with himself. I responded, "I knew that something happened to your wife, but I had no idea you were such a monster, you did that to her as though it was nothing to you as did you not love her? Do you not feel any remorse?" He continued to tell me that it was invigorating; it made him feel alive and made him feel as though he had all the power in the world. I then asked him, "where is your wife now, where did you place her body?" He proceeded to tell me that, just like his house, the land at the cottage was a lot, and during the night he buried each bag each piece of her in different areas and she that nobody would find her. I think my initial shock of everything I just watched, I had suddenly over-come. I thought to myself, is this normal should I be feeling this way should I not be crying hysterically? Maybe what he had shown me was the worst, but now I knew everything he had done to his wife, I knew where the body parts were, and so what are his plans for me? I didn't feel like a victim to him for some reason; instead, I thought he was playing the part of the teacher, and I was his student.

After watching what he had filmed, He then turned to me and said, "You seem to take that better than I expected. Why is that?" I responded "I have no idea, maybe I'm in shock I can't explain it, so now what? What are your plans for me, are you going to do the same to me?" He didn't respond to my question and told me that I would not be sleeping in the house that night; he said that he wasn't ready for me to remain in the home and that I should go back to the barn. I was surprised that he gave me some food to eat, not that I felt like eating, but I know he was putting me in the barn and I had no idea how long I was going to be there by myself. So I ate whatever I could, and at this point, I didn't question what he would give me to drink because part of me just wanted to be asleep, should he drug it, and not witness any more of what was going on, as another part of me wanted to know where the other women were that he killed.

He threw a blanket at me once I was finished eating and drinking, and told me that I might need it which I found rather strange considering I was held captive by him and wondered why he would even give a damn if I was cold or not. He held the chains and guided me to the barn, this time he placed me in a different area I'm not sure why but I was closer to that freezer which I had wondered about since I had been there. This time he hung up a lamp so I had some light, again strange that he would consider giving me a flashlight as well as a blanket, this man who had no remorse after killing his wife cared that he had a sheet and light? There has to be a reason for this, but I was so exhausted from the day and mentally drained after watching the videos that I just wanted to lay down and try and forget, it wasn't easy, and it took me a while to fall asleep; obviously, he hadn't drugged my drink this time either.

I guess I didn't sleep for very long, and when I

woke up, I had the chains as I walked around the area I was in and headed for the freezer. I guess my mind was going to all these crime stories that you see, and you hear about people being murdered and kept in freezers at this point it wouldn't surprise me at all, how I would deal with it, on the other hand, is another question. I took several deep breaths because a large part of me was terrified to find out what was in there, but I had to know. There was enough light in there for me to see but not too clearly. As I opened it I could see food stored in there, but once again my curiosity got the best of me. I began shuffling stuff around until what I feared most I found. I saw an arm, so I moved a few things around to make sure after seeing what he did to his wife if I was just going to find body parts. Well, I was wrong because it was one of the young girls that I had seen him with when I had followed him. Her eyes were open, she was blue, and I jumped back in shock even though I had a strong feeling I would find something or someone in there the entire time I had been held captive. I shut the freezer quickly as I was afraid of what else I might find, and I went back to my spot, but I could not get back to sleep.

Morning finally came, and I just wanted to get out of that barn. I heard the lock opened from the outside and he came in asking me if I had slept well as if he gave a damn. He then asked me "so did you find what you've been looking for ever since you've been here because I know you wanted to see what was in that freezer why do you think I placed you closer to it?" I responded, "You know what I found there, so why are you are asking?" He said, "well, we shall get to that in due time because that's an entirely different story, and besides it's time for breakfast." It was like these crimes were second nature to him as though he had done no wrong, but it had been a long night, I was tired and scared so going into his house seemed much better than where I was during the night in the barn.

Like a dog taken for a walk, he took my chains and walked me into the house and told me if I wanted to wash up, that he would allow it, but the door had to remain open, and of course, the chains had to stay on. Once I was done, he took me to the kitchen had me sit down, put before giving me anything to eat, chuckled to himself and said; "Well, I had a visitor this morning, a police officer, asking if I knew about your whereabouts. They told me that you had been missing and that people from work reported it. Of course, I told them I was shocked and had heard nothing, and hoped that you were all right. I asked if they had notified your family or friends and he responded that you had no family and did not know of any friends, besides the people at work." He proceeded to tell me; "They found your car in the underground parking lot, and there did not seem to be any foul play." I then responded; "You see I told you people would be looking for me." He responded with a laugh; "People are looking for you? The officers told me that you had no family and that apart from the office they could find no friends and that was a nice touch, the car in the underground parking lot makes it a mystery does it not?"

I thought about what he was saying, and I had not told him that I lost my parents in a car accident several years ago, especially when he became of interest to me, I did not want him to know too much about my personal life. Yes, I was a loner, as time went on I became obsessed with him, and what he was doing, so I made excuses when it came to going out with anyone, and slowly people stopped asking me. I had been keeping track of the days by scratching lines on the wall in the barn where I slept, but as time went by I had stopped and had no idea what day it was or how long he had kept me captive. Half of the time I had been drugged, either by the water, he gave me, or possibly something he gave me to eat. I mean, what was I to do, refuse to drink or eat anything? I felt I had no choice, he had me where he wanted, and because of my obsession with him and what he had been doing, I became of interest to him. I wondered to myself, how long the police would look for me, I have seen so many cases go cold, especially during the courses I was taking, articles I read or even on television. I guess even those online courses would just look like it was something I gave up on as I suddenly stopped handing in assignments ever since I had been here. Of course, I thought, what if the police give up on me? After all, there are no signs of foul play in my car, nothing at my apartment that would show I was attacked. In their eyes, I could have just picked up and left to go anywhere, and I didn't know if they would spend too much time looking for me, a missing person that nobody, besides the office. No family, no friends.

I was in a daze after he had told me the police had been there. And to think he wasn't even a person of interest, at least if he were they would have searched his home. He then got my attention and told me to eat; I always wondered why he never called me by my first name but felt he didn't want to as it may show me that he is speaking to me on a more intimate personal level, and being held captive. Well, there was nothing friendly about being held captive; however, it was personal on a different level to me. I then turned to him and said; "Do you even realize I have a first name? It's Annabelle why don't you ever call me by my name?" He just turned, looked at me and looked away, as though it wasn't of any importance to him. Well, I guess there aren't too many serial killers out there who are on a first-name basis with their victims. With his back turned to me, he told me to eat up as we had a big day ahead of us. Is it a big day? I had no idea what he was talking about or what I was in for, but I knew it couldn't be anything pleasant.

While I finished eating, he stepped away for a minute; of course, there was no need for me even to try to see if the door were open, he would always make sure it was locked with his security system. When he came back into the kitchen, he threw a shirt and sweatpants to me and told me to go put them on, they looked like ladies clothing, and I was right. He said to me that he still had some of his wife's dress around. I was led to the bathroom with my chain, where he told me to change. As I put the clothes on, the thought of them belonging to his wife, I was forced to watch, on one of his movies, being cut to pieces, just came back and stuck in my head. It wasn't easy to shake something like that out of my head, never mind the body I had also seen in the freezer. I came out of the bathroom dressed, while he waited anxiously right outside and turned to me with this evil look in his eyes and said; "So I hope you're ready for what we are about to do today, it's going to be a big day for you, something that has been of so much interest." In my head I was thinking, what the hell could this be, I know his crimes have been of interest to me, was this going to be my last day? Was it my turn to become yet another victim of his?

With the chains in hand, he guided me back to the barn and took me to the other side where he had everything so orderly and told me to wait there. I then heard the familiar sound of that damn freezer opening and him fumbling through it. I then heard a sudden thud and the noise of him dragging something. As he came around the corner to my shock, it was the body of the young girl I came across when I looked in that freezer. I asked, still in shock; "What are you doing? Oh my god, she is a human being not a piece of meat. Why are you bringing her in here? Please don't bring her any closer please!" He responded; "Well let's just say, I am your mentor, after all, you have wanted to know what I have been doing for years, now you are going not only to see, you are going to assist me. You do realize that even if you get out of here, you have become an accomplice to murder already. You have watched me, you have seen the women and have said nothing to the police, so don't think you're going to get out of this easy because this is just the beginning." I knew what he was saying was right, for some reason I seemed drawn to him, and what he was doing and I did nothing. I was scared; I never thought I would ever be in this position, becoming a person that looked up to this man as a "mentor", more like his accomplice. I had no idea what he expected me to do, and I was ready to go and dig a grave in the fields on his property, but that's not what he had in mind.

This area of the barn, just like the barn at his cottage in the Hamptons, was very much alike. There was a bench, and this is where he wanted the body of this young girl placed. "You are to help me lift her", he said. Never had I been as close to a dead body even after my parents died in the car accident. It was something I just could not get myself to do. Now I had no choice, as he told me to grab her feet, which were so frozen, for a second, I had forgotten that this was a human being. My hand slipped, and I dropped her feet; my voice had a tremor as I said, "I can't do this, please don't make me do this." He angrily responded; "You will do this, do you understand? You will do as I tell you!" He threw some gloves at my face, which he had on a shelf. It would help with lifting her, I have no idea, and I just did what he said at this point. It was like lifting a heavy table, I didn't want to look, but I had to. You could hear the ice crack, as he wasn't very gentle with her at all while I helped him place her on the bench. I quickly stood as far away from it as I could immediately after doing that with him, more out of fear. He told me that when a body is frozen depending on the tools, it could be quite easy to cut. The best tool to use is a buzz saw, it cuts faster than a chainsaw, and he proceeded to tell me as if I were a medical student. "You are going to assist me as we cut her up, I don't want your lame excuses. You've wanted to know what I do now you can see and learn first hand by assisting me, NOW!" he said, with that evil smirk on his face.

I stood with my back to the wall and watched to see what he was going to do next. Seeing the body laying there brought to mind an article I had read about a woman who left her body for science, wanted it to be frozen, sliced and had given specific instructions. She had given instructions that it should be in thin slices. I found that article rather bizarre, but I guess there are people out there who do have requests regarding their body once they die, leaving specific instructions. However, that article about the women who wanted to be frozen and sliced thin was all I could think of at this time. Then I thought to myself, would it help me if I thought of her as being used for medical reasons. Well, I couldn't as I had seen this young girl alive when I had followed him, and to think I said nothing when she went missing, really struck me hard because maybe I could have somehow prevented it. But who was I kidding; I found some kind of sick excitement in following him and watching his every move before these girls disappeared.

While my mind wandered, distracting me from what he was doing, he yelled at me to pay attention and of course, it all became too real again. And then he began with the buzz saw, and I guess because there was no blood due to how frozen the body was, I was surprised that it prevented me from throwing up. He would stop cutting if I looked away to try and distract myself, and yell to get my attention for him to continue. Suddenly it felt as though I was not looking at a human being anymore, I know how disgusting that sounds, and where were those feelings I had of empathy, why were they no longer there all of a sudden? I felt like I was losing my mind because so many thoughts were going through my mind as I watched him butcher this young girl. Then he told me to grab the large garbage bags he had in his well-stocked shed of death (yes I gave it a name because it was apparent what it was for). As he cut, he told me to hold the large bags open so he could dispose of each piece. I was afraid; however, the thought kept through my mind, why am I still alive?

I thought this entire process would never end, and I felt sick to my stomach. It was over and with a big smile or rather I should say, evil grin, you would think that it was the Thanksgiving turkey he had just finished cutting up then turned to me and said, "Well you know what comes next". Yes, I knew, we would be taking these bags and burying them with all the others, and that is what we did next. I was now his accomplice, but I could not see this getting any easier, I could see no end to this horror, and yet I have to ask myself, is this what I wanted? I know the fascination I had with what he had been doing while working for him would end somehow. Still, I had thought that I would be more of a hero and be able to go to the police with everything I knew and as time went on I just made it worse for myself, so there was no turning back now. Was my life now? And I knew there was no escaping it.

After burying the bags, I felt so dirty in more ways than one, but all I wanted now was to be able to wash this all off me. I asked if I could now take a shower and was wrong. "Now, we eat!" to which I replied; Eat? How could I eat right after that? So; I told him that I wasn't hungry and he still would not let me shower, but instead I had to sit at the table with him, while he ate, I asked for some water, and he continued as though it was just a typical day, and ate while I watched. I was tired, not only physically but also mentally. Once finished he told me to wash the dishes, so I had asked him if I should just put them in the dishwasher, and he abruptly told me, "No, wash them by hand, it's about time that you did some work around here." I thought to myself, have I become not only his accomplice, but his slave as well, but rather than ask any more questions I did what he asked.

He then told me that I could now have the shower, and for the very first time, he removed the chains attached to me. I was shocked but confused as I was still afraid that I might be his next victim. He then told me; "I am taking these chains off as a reward for assisting me today, and you know that you cannot get out of this house, you know that I have a security system that will keep you in here and others out." I knew what he was saying was correct, there was no way out of there, and I could not see me ever having the opportunity to knock him out so I would be able to get out somehow. Still, I had no idea what the security code was, and he had everything necessary under lock and key. He left the bathroom door open while I showered as he always did, but I just wanted to remove all the dirt off me after digging, and part of me wanted to only wash the entire day down the drain so that I would never have to remember it. Unfortunately, that would never happen; the images would remain in my head forever, unfortunately. It was getting rather late, and after my shower, he told me that I could have one of the bedrooms. There was no television, no phone, obliviously, and there was no way for me to open the windows. I was just happy to be given a bed to sleep on finally, however, he did lock me in, but I was okay with that, ultimately being alone meant I could try and be myself, have my thoughts and try to sleep.

I lay there and thought back about my life. I remembered myself as a child, having a normal childhood and playing with other children, being happy and so innocent. My parents, although, strict, gave me a lot of love, something I feel is so essential to any child. I remembered the hugs, laughs, and birthdays I had, all good memories. All these thoughts put some happiness in my mind, something I had not had since I had been here. I then thought of the tragedy of the car accident my parents were in, and how much it affected me. I missed them so much, what I would give to just have one more day with them. Life can be so unfair at times, and we lose the people we love, and I know that's just what life serves us and made me wonder what the families of the girls who went missing must have gone through, especially not even having a body to bury. The police, in my opinion, had a lot of these cases go cold far too soon. I am a missing person, and as I have no family the search for me has not continued as far as I know and told this by this man who I was so very much excited to work for years ago, who I thought made me feel special during the time I did work for him and who now has me captive. I remember when I followed him to these 'dates' with these young women seeing the way he seduced every one of them. Had I let him back then, seduce me the way I felt he was trying to; I may not even be here right now. However, it goes through my mind that I'd rather be dead than be his accomplice, besides why was I so obsessed with him and what he does? Am I sick?

He was supposed to be back today; I had no idea of the time because I didn't have a watch or a clock. I could only tell by day and night. I want to see if I can somehow gain his trust, although that may be an impossible task. I just figured if I'm going captive for god knows how long, I want to be able to have a clock in the room, have a television, be able to read books or newspapers. I think only time will tell and I don't want to bring it up at this point because I am not sure what his plans for me were at this time and I didn't want to make the wrong prematurely. I wondered why he was away for a couple of days. I had no idea if he was still working because he had spent quite some time here, which I assumed was vacation time, it will be interesting to see if he will share that with me.

Well apart from being locked in the room and not being able to go anywhere, I had peace for those two days. I heard a vehicle pull up and looked out of the window, as much as I was able to, and then listened to the door back shut...he was back! It took him a while to come upstairs and check on me, which made me wonder if he had another victim. I'm not sure how long I waited; all I know is that it seemed like forever and that concerned me. I lay on the bed while I waited, chewing on a fingernail, which is not something I usually did, but my nerves got the better of me even though I tried to relax and just breathe.

I then heard the lock on my door, opening, so I quickly sat up because I had no idea what I was to face when the door opened. As the predator stood there with a red face and eyes that looked so evil, which usually meant either anger, he'd been drinking, or he had another victim he may have just brought in. While I sat there wondering he then started telling me "Well, you may just be wondering where I have been the past two days?" I responded, "actually no I didn't, I've just had a lot of time to think because I have no books to read, no television, no computer, and so obviously I know why." He then replied; with that wicked smirk of his, "I have been busy, and ever since questions have been floating around about your disappearance, I thought I would give it some time until it seemed like the police made it a cold case. I have decided to take early retirement; this way, I can focus on me, what I love the most, and have time to know what I am going to do with you." He continued to tell me that he and brought up his early retirement during the time of these missing girls, he said that's what led him to make the plan of getting me here. He went on, as though I were a personal friend of his and cared that his retirement party went so well, which was planned much earlier before his plan of keeping me here. The bank asked him what date would be best. I'm not quite sure about all the details because he just rambled on, while I thought to myself that my living hell with him was now going to get worse with all the time he had on his hands. In the back of my mind, I kept telling myself I have to try and gain his trust. While he rambled on, I offered to make dinner this evening and was quite shocked when he said to me that I could. As it was the first time, he agreed to let me cook, as he has always put whatever it was in front of me, usually sandwiches, and made me eat. I tried to remain calm and put on a pleasant persona, something I will have to force myself to do until I get a little more freedom in that house.

He locked the door again, as he wanted to change his clothes, but to make sure he knew where I was, this is something I want to stop happening, but I can't push my luck. He unlocked my door, told me to come into the kitchen and showed me where everything I would need to cook was. The kitchen was always well stocked with food, and it made me wonder how many others were held captive here before me. He didn't have too much to say so I kept my mouth shut, as it wasn't the time to get friendly and just cooked a simple meal, something I was hoping that I would get to eat, as well as him. Once it was ready, I just stood there until I knew what I should be doing next. Surprisingly he told me to sit down and join him and so I did. It was the first proper meal I had since being there. Once done, I had to take care of the dishes, while he sat back and watched after making himself, what seemed to be a rather strong drink. He told me that once to go to my room upstairs when I finished. I was happy to do that knowing that I felt safe in there, it had a bathroom and everything I needed, and I looked forward to hopefully having a good sleep.

I was surprised at how well everything went once he came home, and I was so relieved that he did not return with yet another victim. He wasn't nasty, but when I saw him drinking after dinner, I did get concerned, as his violent side seemed to come out, as I had seen quite often while being held here. After a while, what seemed like hours, I heard him thumping up the stairs yelling out my name? I quickly got under the covers and pretended I was asleep, hoping that he would just lock the door. Unfortunately, I was wrong and felt threatened by the tone of his voice. He grabbed hold of my blanket and threw it aside. Apart from drugging me, he had never hurt me in any way, not physically anyway; mentally, I will never get what I had witnessed out of my mind. He made damn sure I was awake and knelt on top of me, put his hands around my neck, and began to squeeze and kept repeating, "How do you like this Annabelle?" I was helpless, I couldn't breathe, and I had no strength to push him off. Was this it? Was I going to die tonight? And then he eased off around my throat and laughed like a mad man while I tried to breathe, as I couldn't speak at this point. He then proceeded to tell me, "you see Annabelle, and this is how I take the life out of anyone I want, but I'm not ready to do that to you, (as he laughed in his evil way) oh no, I have plans for you". At that point, when I got my breath back, I pleaded with him not to hurt me; I told him I would do anything. I wish I kept my mouth shut, but I was scared. One of my worst fears then happened. He proceeded to rape me violently for what seemed like an eternity, and once done, he just left me lying there as he locked me in the room. That night I cried myself to sleep as I was in too much pain to move from the bed and wash his filth off me.

Once morning came, I still cried to myself, I was in pain but made my way to the bathroom as I felt so dirty and could still smell his alcohol breath from last night. As I showered, I cried and didn't realize how much he had hurt me. The bruises, the bites he made, and a mark still around my neck. I'm not sure what's going to happen to me next. Was he done with me? Part of me wished he were done with me, as at this point I just wanted to die. Once showered, I put some clothes on and sat on my bed in fear.

I then heard him unlocking my door, and he behaved as though nothing had happened and told me to come downstairs with him to the kitchen. I hung my head in shame and sauntered, as I was still hurting. He suggested we have breakfast, I told him that I wasn't hungry; however, he even expected to make him something to eat, which is what I did along with a cup of coffee for myself. I sat at the table, as he and I said; "We have to do some serious talking if you want to live, do you understand". I nodded, yes. I didn't ask what it was we had to discuss, because at this point I felt sick to my stomach after what happened last night, and having to sit next to him as though nothing had happened. So, I just let him do the talking. He proceeded to say; "If you expect to live, you're gonna do whatever it is that I want and expect from you, and if you don't, you can expect to join the others in the field, have I made myself clear?" Once again, I nodded as tears came down my face. "Stop crying", he said abruptly, as I tried to wipe the tears off my face and tried to contain myself. He continued to talk and said, "Now that I have more time on my hands, for me things are going to be much easier. I'm keeping you here, but I'm not sure what my plans are for you yet. You brought a lot of unnecessary attention toward me by law enforcement, detectives, and people in the office, and that has me furious. You wanted to know what I did, now you know, and you're just lucky I didn't kill you last night! But I'll tell you one thing; I enjoyed last night, you have no idea how long I've wanted to do that to you." At this point, I was numb and did not respond in any way to him. He proceeded to say; "During the time I've had you here I have cleared my name for any suspicion about you going missing, and I was lucky they didn't dig any deeper into my past and present life. I hope everything you have done has been worth your while because now you're going to pay in more ways than one. Go upstairs to your room and stay there until I let you out."

I made my way up, and I heard him follow me and lock the door. In one way, I was relieved to be back in this room alone, but on the other hand, so many thoughts were going through my mind about what plans he had in store for me. I couldn't stop crying and covered my mouth so that he didn't hear me as I sobbed. I kept telling myself that I had to compose myself and find the strength within me because I needed to show him that I was able to handle what I was going through and that I was able to stand up for myself. Unfortunately, I think I had a long road ahead of me for that to happen. I kept wondering if the other girls had gone through what I had. I know when I was keeping track of the disappearances; most of them found murdered, had not been missing for as long as I have. I know most of the women were strangled. And I do believe they were all raped. He was more of a monster than I had imagined because he had a graveyard of his very own on his property for so many others, many of which I had not heard about, but helped him dispose of them. What have I become?

When I was in my room, I took a look in the mirror and could barely recognize the person I saw or was it me seeing what I felt I had become? I washed my face as I had done so much crying, my face looked like I had aged and I felt so dirty inside.

I decided to have a shower, and while doing so, I sat down in the bathtub holding my knees close to my body and let the water just run all over it, as I sobbed but tried to cover my mouth as I didn't want to draw any attention to myself for him to come in. I don't think I could ever feel clean or like myself ever again. Everything I had gone through so far had changed me as a person in a way that I really can't explain. I felt the need to write my feelings down, but I know if I asked him for a pen and paper, he would be suspicious of me for one reason or another. As I got out of the bathtub, I could see the bruises all over my body, which were constant reminders. I covered myself in shame, changed into some clean clothes so that I could just lie down. I tried to close my eyes, but the images of what he did to me kept me awake, and I was so scared that he might come in at any time.

After a restless night, I had awoken to a bang on the bedroom door which startled me and heard him say; "Get yourself dressed we have things to discuss, and I will unlock the door in 15 minutes, be ready!" I barely had time to wash my face, brush my teeth and just put whatever clothes I had near me, on. When I looked in the mirror, I couldn't believe how hollow I looked. I heard him unlocking the door and sat ready, as though I was a child, for him to tell me what to do. He doesn't deserve a name; he's a monster. He told me to make my way to the kitchen table and sit down. He didn't ask to make breakfast; had something far more critical to say to me, and what followed shocked me.

He began telling me about a new plan he has for 'us'…he proceeded to say; "You are going to learn what it is like to be me because you're going to help me get my next victim. That's what you were interested in, correct? He wasn't waiting for an answer but was just making a point because of my curiosity with him. He then continued; "I have been giving some thought to what kind of girl, woman, or whatever you want to refer to them as. I was thinking along the lines of a schoolgirl; because there is a particular school, I have had my eye on; then again, to make it easier I think a whore would be much easier to get with the both of us present. I don't want you squirming and making the entire process fail and draw attention to us." Following that, all he said was, "now make breakfast, and this time eat. All I need is a frail accomplice on my hands to worry about". He just kept rambling on about all this, and I had no idea if he was talking to himself, me, or maybe an alter ego.

I never said a word; I was in shock to think how soon he was getting another victim and including me in his plans. I felt numb and proceeded to make whatever it was he told me to, and although I felt sick to my stomach, I had to force myself to eat and drink something. I remained quiet, trying not to listen to him too much because he was freaking me out in more ways than one at this point. I seriously was wondering who the hell he was talking to, I mean he was a psychopath but could he be one with multiple personalities? The more I thought about it, the more it made sense. I could see how he could be that businessman without any signs of a personality disorder, managing an entire department as one of the head executives. Then I could see how he could become the seducer to convince women of how genuine and trusting he was to them, (and that would include me) before my suspicions. There was the paedophile, the way he stalked young girls from schools. I saw the evil in him; the real psychopath, and I wondered how many more identities he may have. Of course hoping one of them had empathy, as maybe with that personality if I had the opportunity, I could find a way out of this hell which he had put his grasp over me. I went into a daydream somewhat, going over everything in my head to see if what I thought about him could be right about him having these personalities. The more I thought, the more it made sense.

I was suddenly startled, as he grabbed hold of my arm and he demanded; "I hope you are listening to everything I'm saying, you seem to be in a world of your ...pay attention!!" As he still had a tight hold of my arm, he dragged me through his hallways as he had to show me something to prove how serious he was about this plan of his, and that I'd better not do anything to jeopardize his plan. He was hurting me, but I knew I couldn't say anything. When he opened the door to this room I was shocked to see that he had various guns (they looked like they were on show for more than just being a collector) and confirmed it when he said to me; "You see those? They have all been used to kill. So try anything when we do get out of this house to get 'our', next victim, and I will not hesitate to use one of them on you." I thought to myself, I have never hurt anyone in my life, never mind the thought of killing someone. Another cabinet had sexual torture gadgets, which he smirked as he told me how he enjoyed using them. Then he showed me several Tasers he had in his possession and warned me that those would come in handy to remind me of my place and what I was to do. To show me the strength of one, he held it towards my neck, and I fell to the ground and blacked out.

I woke up with him slapping my face to get up, but my body still felt tensed up and in pain, how the hell did he expect me to get up after that which made my muscles seize up. It was his way or the even harder way! I slowly tried to get up, collapsing a couple of times, so he grabbed my arm hard and told me to get to my feet. His anger scared me even more so now after seeing all these weapons he had that I had no choice but to force myself up. He then told me that if I don't do what he tells me, to expect punishment, and that he had only given me a taste of it. His tone seemed so different from what I had heard in previous conversations; it was scary, and I knew what he told me was very real. There is no way I could even think of trying to escape at this point also if I had the opportunity. From what he has been telling me he has a plan for both of us to go out one night to an area, which I guess was quite familiar to him; to pick up a prostitute and I was to be involved in capturing this young person, he made that very clear to me. He then went on talking, (as though he was talking to himself...maybe another alter ego), however, it could have been meant for me to hear. He was going to take a drive on his own first because he wanted to pick the right one. Whether I liked it or not, I had no choice to be part of this if I wanted to stay alive. Before he left, he made sure to remind me that there was no way of getting out of the house, he had made sure of this. I had access to only what was in my room, and that is where he was going to leave me while he left to pick his prey. As I heard the key locking my door, I knew that this was a new chapter of my life that was going to begin, and although the thought of it scared me, it did cause me some curiosity, but I could not control this feeling for some reason. I mean I was here, I have assisted him with some girls he had already murdered in the past, to dispose of them, so at this point, and I could either be a victim or an accomplice. What would you pick if you were in this situation?

He drove to one of the worst areas downtown, which he was quite familiar with. He drove slowly just as a predator making sure the one he picked was to his liking. He stopped and asked the group of women who stood with her "are you here every day at this spot?" One of them replied," "Yes, are you looking for something? Between all of us, we can do anything you want, and why not now, why are you waiting? You don't know what you're missing, sugar." He replied, "Oh, I know what I want and what I'm looking for." As he drove off, he glanced around the area, just making sure of the surroundings for when he came back, and it was a neglected area, with not too many people around almost hidden, the perfect space for him not to be seen or recognized. There was one girl who stood out who was young with dark hair that looked like a schoolgirl, and he had already decided that she would be his next victim.

When he returned, he didn't unlock my door right away, but once opened, began telling me about where he had been and described what his next victim was. He also added that I should prepare myself because there was not going to be anything said to anyone while we were out, that he would do all the talking, and that he would have a gun right beside him at all times. I don't know how many times he has reminded me that I should try and scream, talk, or make myself stand out in any way that he would not hesitate to shoot me. I mean, what does he think, I've been here for god knows how long, and I see what he is capable of, why would I even try to make a wrong move.

He then left me in the room, and I could hear him talking to himself once again, almost as if he was speaking to one of his alter egos. I could hear him say, "Ok, you saw the one I want next...so what's the plan? What do you mean? I know what I'm going to do; I may enjoy her a little before I decide whether I skin her alive, something new, that's right!!" It was almost as though he had another person with him discussing his plan, and then I heard that evil laugh. I had seen some of his work on the other girls he had murdered, but skinning someone was not his usual way of conspiring to kill his victim, and the thought of it made me feel sick, especially as I was going to have to be involved.

The times I had in my room, I mean, I may as well call it that now, I watched a lot of documentaries about crime, shows, and movies to do with murder and a lot of psychological thrillers. They have always appealed to me for many years, and I don't believe it's abnormal to do so, except when watching them now, I do believe it was a way of me trying to place myself as the murder. I mean, I wanted to know how it would feel to have that power over someone, being the person to decide whether they live or die, the methods, practices, and cautions one would take. A lot of the shows I watched would show the mentality of the murderer. And it wasn't always related to how they were raised or treated as a child. They just thrived on committing the crimes they committed, and most did it literally without a reasonable doubt. Putting myself in their place wasn't easy, however, as I had already taken part in helping my captor to dismember several of his past victims, I did feel that I could face a crime again...or could I?

I think his mentality was rubbing off on me, or he had brainwashed me in some way. Regardless, I knew I would have no say or choice in the next murder, which he had planned, and I cannot describe what I feel. I can't imagine what part he wants me to play in his plan because all he has told me is that I am going to be there with him. At this point, I was doing what, as asked, I had food; I had a decent place to sleep and he found enough trust not to lock the bedroom door when he was there. However, there was still no way of getting out of that house. The evening came; I had eaten, bathed and spent most of the day in my room. The last thing he had said to me was to be ready for tomorrow night, and that was it. My mind was working overtime, I wasn't one to bite my nails, but found myself doing so due to not knowing what I was going to face tomorrow, and as far as sleep, I don't know if I was going to get any.

The night seemed to fly by and if I did sleep it wasn't very much at all. I did my usual routine, as I did every morning, unless I was told otherwise, and waited for him to come and unlock the door to go downstairs for breakfast. Well, I guess there was not going to be any breakfast because he did not come and open the door. I began chewing my nails again, while I waited. I then lay back down on the bed, as I had no idea what was going on. I guess a few hours had passed and I heard the lock open on my door and he said; "You can come downstairs now and make us some sandwiches." I never asked him why he did not come and get me in the morning; I proceeded to make the sandwiches, something to drink and sat at the table, where he then joined me. I didn't want to talk, but my mind was working overtime. Then he said; "As soon as it gets dark tonight, I shall get everything ready. I want you to remain in your room and I will only call on you when I am ready. I will not repeat your part in this again; I believe I have made myself clear and as I have stated to you already, you will be blindfolded and your hands will be tied when we leave this house." I just nodded as he proceeded to tell me to go back to my room.

As soon as it started getting dark outside, my heart was beating profoundly, not knowing how this plan of his was going to turn out. This room had become my cell, and I had become used to it. However, the thought of getting out of this house was the only thing I was looking forward to, even though I was going to be blindfolded. I had been writing my thoughts down on a book he had given me, something I asked for, which surprisingly he had agreed. It was the right way of releasing a lot of my feelings. He read the book whenever he wanted to, so I had to be cautious of what I wrote down. I also used to draw in the book; it gave me something to do. It's incredible when you are confined to a room, what talents you had no idea you had just come out.

I guess we were not going to have dinner either, as it seemed forever that I was up in my room. I began to wonder if this man had changed his mind but was doubtful. Time had passed, and he came in, took me by the arm, and walked me downstairs. He then tied my hands behind my back and blindfolded me. He told me that he had everything he needed in the car and proceeded to walk me to the garage. I guess it was open as I felt the warm fresh air against my face for a few seconds before putting me into the backseat of his car. I thought to myself how I had taken nature and being outside for granted, how much I never really appreciated it. I now just longed for it and wished I could go out and enjoy it. I also wondered if that time would ever come.

As he drove, there was silence for a while,

and while being blindfolded, my mind wandered, imagining what life was like before being held captive, remembering only the right things. The drive seemed interminable, and I had no idea where we were going apart from what he had told me. He had tied my hands behind my back, which made the drive uncomfortable, but at least it wasn't too tight. I'm sure my comfort was the last thing on his mind. All of a sudden, the silence was broken as he began telling me what my part in this would be. He said that once we reached our destination, he would park on a side street where he would blindfold me and untie my restraints. But he warned me that should I make one wrong move that he would not hesitate to put me out of my misery, and I believed him. He then said that once he did that, we would then drive to this impoverished area where the young girl he had preyed would be. He told me that once we got there, he would invite her into the car, and my job while driving would be to reach around and smother her with chloroform, which he had soaked a cloth with and placed by my feet. Don't get me wrong, the thought of just covering his mouth with chloroform came to mind, but he was too smart to try anything, and his strength would overcome mine.

Once he prepared me, we then drove around the corner, where it was a pretty dark and isolated area, but I guess I was well known for those who were looking for prostitutes. He stopped at the side of the road, where several girls were standing around, and one approached the car, so he rolled the window down enough to speak, but not seen, as he had tinted windows so that nobody could see me either. This particular girl said, "are you looking for some company tonight?" He responded,' "No thanks, but can you get me the girl standing against the wall, the young girl with the long black hair?" She then turned away from the car, and we could see her speaking to the girl in question, who then made her way over to the car, and she then said; "I believe you were asking about me, what can I do for you tonight?" By the way, she spoke I could t with her soft insecure voice, this was very new to her, being so young and seeing her adjusting her clothes, in particular, as I saw her tugging on the short skirt she had on, which lead me to believe that she wasn't at all what she was attempting to be. I remained silent in the back of the car as he replied to her, "Well yes, I have seen you here before, and I would like you to join me for the evening and don't worry, the price is irrelevant, I will pay whatever you want." She looked back at the other girls, as he unlocked the front passenger door and let her in. After she got in, he quickly closed the car window, locked the automatic doors, which of course, he was in control of and began to drive. I don't believe she had ever seen me, as I stayed silent in the back seat. She then said, "My name is Sara, so where are we going?" He responded, "For now, I would like you just to stay silent, as I am driving to my home. No need to be concerned, you're going to enjoy this."

She had put her seatbelt on, and remained silent, as he had asked. He had told me before picking her up, that once she was in the car, he would give me the okay by looking in the rearview mirror with a nod when it was time for me to cover her mouth with chloroform, So I kept my eyes peeled on the rearview mirror once we began to drive. I know he wanted me to do this while we were in this area, as it was pretty desolate. I then saw him stare at me with a nod, and when I say stare, there was evil in his eyes.

I bent down quietly, held the chloroform soaked cloth with both hands, raised myself above the passenger seat, and very quickly placed it over her face and pulled as tight as I could from the back seat, as she struggled and tried to pull it off, I felt her fear. It didn't take as long as I thought it would, and she sat there lifeless for the remainder of the drive back to his house. He had beside him not only the gun but also the Taser in case she woke up. I felt the gun was there for me, as he had warned me should I do anything besides what he told me to do; he wouldn't hesitate to use it. The remainder of the drive, there was absolute silence.

Once we arrived, he drove directly to the barn where he had kept me. The young girl began to move around a bit, and he did not hesitate to tase her before we did anything else. Her body shook as though she was having a seizure, and then she went limp. He then instructed me to help him get her in the barn, and I did as told, and we placed her in an area he had set up to keep her. He then had me help him restrain her with ropes tying her arms behind her back tightly and also around her ankles. He had set up a blanket on the floor for her. However, he didn't speak about what his plans for her were going to be. At this point, all the triggers of when I was there came back. I could only imagine what she was going to go through. Before we made our way out of the barn, he stroked her hair and then made his way down her legs and, while feeling her said, "I'll be back to take care of you."

While he had that evil smirk on his face, we made our way out of there, and he locked it so that should she wake up, there was nowhere she could go. He then told me to get back in the car and drove to the house and put the car in the garage. He just wanted to get me back in my room, and before he locked the door, he said, "you did a good job." Was that supposed to make me feel proud of what I had done? Or was this his way of letting me know that I should expect to be involved in more as though I had become his partner in his crime. It was late; I was tired and decided to wash what I had done by taking a shower and trying my best not to think of what I was going to be involved in next. I then changed and got into bed, working hard to fall asleep.

It was as though the night flew by when I heard him opening the door and telling me abruptly, "hurry up and get dressed and come downstairs." I did, and when I got downstairs, he ordered me to get something for the girl in the barn to eat and drink. I guess this meant there was no time for me this morning, as it's usually me who comes down to eat breakfast. Regardless, once I prepared something, he told me to walk ahead of him, and we walked to the barn, he opened the barn door, and this young girl was looking extremely scared. I forgot her name at this point, but at the same time, I really didn't want to make myself familiar with her, for I had no idea what was to become of her, so remained one of her captors.

As I lay the food down on the floor, he told me to untie her hands only, so I did, not saying a word. He stepped away outside the barn for a few minutes, so I bent down and talked to her very quietly and said; "I have been where you are now if you don't you will die, do you understand?" She didn't say a word but just stared at me, so I continued, "Here is something for you to eat and drink, If you don't want it, it will be your loss, as he will punish you and not give you anything until he decides. He is in charge here, don't speak unless he asks you to, you don't have a choice, do you understand? Don't think you can escape because you can't, we are in the middle of nowhere, and besides, he will have his eyes on you at all times. One wrong move, and yes, you're dead." I said that to her with a stern voice to try and make her understand. She still said nothing. When he came back in, she looked up at him in despair not knowing what to expect, as he brushed her hair away from her face saying; "You are a beautiful young girl, and if you do as I say you will stay that way, if not, you'll end up out there in that field where I will bury you." He said this as he pointed to the area we had buried the other victims.

She didn't want to eat, but I made sure she drank some water at least; I then asked her if she needed to use the bathroom and before I could finish what I was saying he stopped me and said; "She's not doing anything until I get the chains on her, you know the procedure." he said as he threw the chains by my feet. I began to untie the rope around her ankles and replaced it with the chain. With this done, I then led her as I was, like a dog, to that outhouse in the barn and allowed her to close the door as I held on to the chains which were attached to her still. I then walked her back to the blanket, told her to sit while I chained her wrists, and made sure she was unable to get out. He just stood there and had that evil smirk on his face as to approve everything I was doing. He then told her that he would be back, so we both left the barn as he locked it and made our way to the main house, where he took me up to my room and locked the door.

As I sat in my room, thoughts ran through my mind, wondering what was I to him now? This girl was much younger, was she my replacement and if so, what would be my fate. I heard him downstairs as he seemed to leave the house, so I ran to my window and saw him making his way to the barn, and I could only imagine what he was going to do next. He seemed to be in there forever, and as he began walking back to the house, he was zipping up his pants and doing up his belt buckle. I just knew that he had raped her, which gave me more to worry about because I was his go-to woman while I was here when he wanted sex. If it was up to his satisfaction, where did that leave me? I hated his forceful sex, so my concern was what did he have planned for me? I heard him coming up the stairs and unlocking my door, he looked messed up and sweaty and just casually told me that I was now allowed to come down and eat something. He then told me once I was done, I was to go back to the barn because we needed to clean her up.

Once done, we walked over to the barn to find this girl sobbing and holding her knees to her chest tightly. So yes, she had been raped. As he stood there supervising, I got a bowl of water and a towel and wiped her down. She fought me as I tried to get her to let go of her knees, but I needed to clean her up as she was also bloody, and I looked up at him in disgust. When he raped me, it was extremely violent, and it was obvious that what she had experienced was what I had gone through. Once done, she lay down, curled up like an infant. He told me to hurry up as he wanted to relax. Seriously? But that was the type of person he was so it shouldn't have surprised me.

When we went back to the house as always, he took me to my room, but I noticed that he locked me in again, just when I thought I was getting somewhere to have him trust me. Having this young girl became his priority, and once again, I just had to be patient. All this was all too much for me and was exhausting, mentally. So I just lay down on the bed and eventually fell asleep.

I'm not sure how long I had fallen asleep for, but it was still daylight outside, and I heard him go in and out of the house at least two more times before it got darker outside. I tried the door to see if he had unlocked it, but now it was not. I began feeling frustrated and angry and not scared anymore. I had to think of what might be, should he not want me anymore, and how could I avoid this. I had been here all this time, how the hell was I going to escape that now?

Days turned into weeks, doing the same thing day after day; some days, the girl was in pretty bad shape, she had been beaten, raped, and the chains on her wrists and ankles had become bloody. He seemed to keep her in there longer than I thought he would. In the meantime, I was spending most of my time in my 'cell' of a room, not knowing what was going to happen from day to day. I did know that I was becoming bitter, and even angrier as time went on but couldn't show that to him. The fact that the girl was still alive told me that he had no intention of getting rid of her in a hurry. So in my head, I began to think of what I would do if given the opportunity, and how much he did not know about me. He had me cooking meals while he was in the house, where he could watch over me, so I didn't have any time on my own in that house since this girl had been there, and he made sure if I wasn't with him that I was locked in my room. The frustration kept growing, and my mind was working overtime with various plans if ever I had the opportunity to follow through.

On this specific day, with evening approaching, he let me out of my room to come to have dinner, which I needed as I had not been down to have anything all day. He seemed agitated, so I kept my mouth shut because I had no idea what the hell was going on. He was talking to himself, I'm assuming another one of his alter egos, and there was an angry conversation. He began pacing as I prepared myself something to eat, and as I sat down, he said, "Okay, that was not supposed to happen, I wanted her, damn it!" He then looked at me and said, "You know what we have to do now? And this wasn't supposed to happen, but she'll have to go."

I finally asked him what he was talking about and to my surprise he told me that she wasn't breathing, I asked; "You are speaking about the girl in the barn?" and he replied, "Well of course, whom else do you think I'm talking about? Things just went too far; she struggled when I specifically told her not to, and I had to stop her from crying." At that time, I knew that he had strangled her, as this was something he would even do when he raped me. Although I felt some remorse for her, at the same time, I was relieved, as maybe this meant I was not going to be the victim. He continued to say rather frantically, "We have to take care of this, and not tonight tomorrow, do you hear? And then we have to go back and get another." Then his face went from angry to that creepy smirk as he continued, "I do have another in mind, and she'll do nicely, we'll just have to go over all the plans tomorrow after we remove the girl from the barn." To him, it was like picking out a new toy because the old one had broken. After talking, he told me that it was time for me to go up to my room because he was exhausted. And so I did, but this time I did not hear him lock my door. I placed my ear to the door and heard him walking to his room and shut the door, and then I waited for an hour or so because I had a plan. I very quietly opened my door and crept up to his bedroom door, and I could hear him snore.

Now, I had to do a few things before I went to see if this girl was dead for sure. I very quietly crept down the stairs, and I went to the room with all his guns, which was on the main floor. To my luck, it, he had become extremely absent-minded, and that was to my advantage. I picked a gun, made sure it was loaded; then I looked for the handcuffs he had used on me in the past, which was also in that room. I grabbed them along with a flashlight and then went to check the alarm, he always said he had it on, but it wasn't. Next, I had to grab the key to the barn's lock, which he had hanging in the kitchen. Rather than go through the front door, I made my way through the kitchen and quietly opened the door to go outside from there.

I then ran to the barn making sure my flashlight was on and proceeded to open the barn. I saw the young girl lying there on the floor covered in blood, I pointed the flashlight on her, felt her pulse, she died. He had not only strangled her but had done it with a rope with great force as I could see the bad ligature marks on her neck. I couldn't really do anything for her, so quickly made my way back to the house and quietly made my way back inside, trying extremely hard not to make a sound. I had left the gun and the handcuffs on the floor, and I grabbed them and made my way up the stairs this time using the flashlight and made my way to his room.

It was my opportunity, and I was ready. I had a rag and doused it with chloroform. As I opened the door slowly making my way to his bed, and with two hands, I put the rag over his face, and I was lucky he was asleep at the time; if not, I would have had a struggle. Once he was out, I quickly got the handcuffs, rolled him over face down and handcuffed his hands behind his back and tied his ankles tight. I then rolled him on to his back again because when he woke up, I wanted him to see me standing there and made sure to gag him as I was going to be the one talking this time, not him. I was in no rush, so I gathered everything I needed before getting out of that damn house. But before I left, I had something I wanted to tell him, which I am sure will come as quite a surprise.

I sat and watched him as the time passed by, remembering everything he had done to me until I finally saw some movement as he awoke. I had some water in a glass and threw it on his face, slapping him a few times to make sure he was fully awake and aware of who was in control at this time, me!

I stood there with my hands on my hips and a smile on my face and said, "Well, are we awake? Because you need to listen to what I have to say." It sounds of him trying very hard to speak; I ignored it because that gag was staying where it was. I showed him the gun I had loaded, stuck in near his head a few times to hopefully make him fearful, as I smiled and continued to speak. "Well, I waited for you to slip a few times, and you didn't disappoint. You left my bedroom door open, the security system unarmed, and keys hanging where I could find them." I said as I laughed to ridicule him.

I continued, "You have no idea who I am and how long I have waited to share a little of my past with you," he lay there helplessly staring at me. "You see, the innocence that I portrayed was just an act I had practiced most of my life, and I think I did it rather well, wouldn't you say? My parents were pretty strict with me, so I did as they asked, but while I did, I came across an article on you, which you might say, I became quite obsessed with. You see I had quite an interest in serial killers, murders, and death as a whole, so I have spent a lot of time studying you and figuring out ways of how I could get closer to you, and although it took a lot of time and effort, it was worth it, because looks where I am now." I laughed, as I played around with the gun, rubbing it around his face as I spoke.

"As far as my poor parents, well, their terrible accident was not exactly that. You see, I arranged for their car to be compromised, which led to their death. Yes, it was sad, after all, they did raise me, not exactly the way I would have liked, however, I knew that, once they were out of the picture, financially I would be okay, they made sure of that in their will. Yes, I know that was just a bonus! However, it was more than I expected and will be able to live quite a comfortable life.

I paid many people to do my research on you, and others I paid to find you and made sure that I would work with you eventually. It's amazing what people will do for the right amount of money, with no questions asked. Of course, I had to make it all look extremely real, which meant working jobs I couldn't stand, but it was worth the sacrifice. I mean, it led me to you, and your seduction was right on point, you fell for my flirtation, and you were quite disgusting."

I was speaking as I paced the floor of his bedroom, ignoring his efforts to speak. "So you see, we do have something in common, I also love the kill, and probably have since I was a child." His eyes showed me that he was in shock to hear of my past, and now that the shoe was on the other foot, I am sure he felt some kind of fear, even though he was such an evil man himself. I continued to speak to him. "As far as that poor young girl in the barn, well sadly you had already made sure she was dead, however, that's one last thing I have to do. You will suffer, I will make sure of it, and I do feel I will get a lot of satisfaction from this leaving no trace that I was ever here. Considering the police have stopped looking at me quite a while ago and presume that I am dead, I have nothing to worry about. I have big plans for myself, you see, oh, and if it's okay with you, I will be taking your car to get to my next destination". I laughed knowing, of course, he had no say in anything I was about to do.

There was a large container of gasoline in the garage and a couple of small tanks of propane. I brought in the tanks of propane and placed one of them by the front door. I then brought in the container of gasoline; found some matches by the fireplace. I placed them in my pocket, while I got the car keys and drove the car, leaving it further down the driveway for my quick getaway. I thought of setting the barn on fire, but thought twice because he had killed the girl there. I wanted the police to find her to make it look like he planned what was about to happen to him and his home.

The gasoline container was heavy, but the adrenaline rush I had made the container feel as though it were practically empty.

I then entered his room and said, "I guess you have an idea what I am going to do next? But the pain should not last too long before you die, you son of a bitch!" His eyes were wide with fear, and I could see the sweat on his brow, I mean, what did he think I was going to do, leave him laying there for someone to find him? I want to make sure this house goes up in flames, but I also want an explosion so that there will not be too much of him left or that they will not be able to identify the body. After that, I don't care because; I made sure my plans for my future were already taken care of. I went and brought the other propane tank and put it in his room.

Slowly I poured the gasoline first over him and his bed, then around the room, while he attempted to scream with the gag on his mouth, and I made sure to smile before I left him there. I then continued pouring it along the hallway to the room I was locked in, then poured some down the stairs into the living room, kitchen, and finally ended at the front door. The kitchen's side door was open, so I decided to light a match and start the fire from there rather than the entrance where the propane tank was. It would give me enough time to run down the driveway to the car before anything exploded, and I could drive away before emergency vehicles got there, which would take a while, as he was in the middle of nowhere.

As the house began to burn, and I made my way to the car, and as I began to drive away, I turned one last time to take a look at the house and smiled. As I drove, I knew I would be okay, as my money was transferred to an account at a bank under my new name. Also, my plan included a change in my identity, which was already all taken care of. I had all the documents, including a driver's license, passport, etc. in a safety deposit box at this bank. A majority of my inheritance already was wired to a bank in the Cayman Islands. That would be my final destination.

The plan was going smoothly, and I had made sure I dressed accordingly not to make anything look suspicious, and damn I looked good! I parked his car a couple of blocks away from the bank, as planned, and walked to the bank where I would start my new life. Was I going to get the urge to kill again? Time would only tell.

ABOUT *the* AUTHOR

Michele Gmitrowski was born in Calcutta, India, but raised in the United Kingdom from the age of four. When she was sixteen, she and her family immigrated to Canada, where she still lives today. Her heritage is a mixture of Spanish, Irish, Armenian, and British.

As a child, Ms. Gmitrowski was a tomboy—always playing soldiers with the neighborhood kids, and loving to write detective stories as a pastime. As she grew older, she became a lover of poems, and eventually had one of her own published in 2004, in *VoicesNet Anthology*.

She also had a book published in 2019, "The Darkness Within" by Inkwater Press, her memoir.

Ms Gmitrowski is happily married and has two wonderful children from a previous marriage (a son and a daughter), as well as three grandchildren, and a third on the way. Her family makes her feel quite blessed.